"Daddy! Mother!" howled Freddie. "Catch him! Save me!"

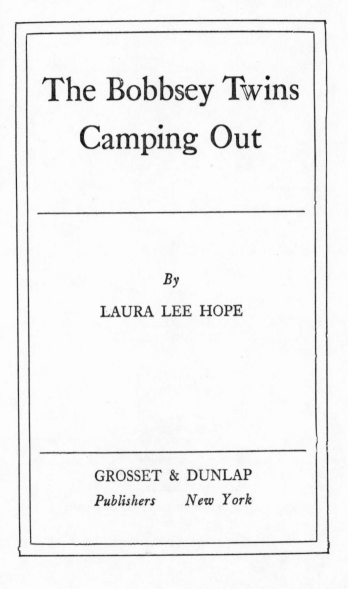

The Bobbsey Twins
Camping Out

By

LAURA LEE HOPE

GROSSET & DUNLAP
Publishers   New York

ISBN: 0-448-08016-8

PRINTED IN THE UNITED STATES OF AMERICA

The Bobbsey Twins Camping Out

CONTENTS

CHAPTER I

A WILD TALE

"DAD has a secret!" twelve-year-old Nan Bobbsey whispered in the ear of her twin brother Bert. The dark-haired, brown-eyed boy, who looked very like Nan, was idly swinging in a hammock stretched between two trees in the front yard.

"A secret?" exclaimed Bert, sitting up so suddenly that he nearly fell out of the hammock.

"Hush!" exclaimed Nan, motioning toward Flossie and Freddie, the younger twins of the Bobbsey family. The blond six-year-olds were in another part of the yard digging a hole. "Don't let them hear you, Bert, or they'll ask what the secret is. And I don't know it myself," Nan added with a laugh.

"Then how do you know it's a secret?" asked Bert.

He moved to one end of the hammock to make room for Nan. No sooner had she sat down than both she and Bert fell with a thump to the ground.

Luckily, there was plenty of thick, green grass beneath the hammock, which had been put in place only that day. Scuffling feet had not yet destroyed the turf.

"Oh, see what you did!" cried Nan as she stared at the broken rope.

"Me?" Bert laughed, and teased, "It was your great weight, Nan, that—"

"Okay," Nan said. "Only you're heavier than I am."

The sound of their fall brought Flossie and Freddie on the run.

"Oh, how funny you look!" cried Flossie, shaking her golden curls and giggling.

"Do it again so we can watch you!" begged Freddie, his blue eyes, just like those of Flossie, shining with eagerness.

"Do it again? Not me!" exclaimed Bert, as he scrambled to his feet and helped Nan to rise. "I gave my elbow a hard whack."

"And I think my knee is skinned," added Nan. In Bert's ear she whispered, "Don't say anything about the secret."

"How can I when I don't know what the secret is and you don't either?" he asked.

"Hush!" whispered Nan, but it was too late. The sharp ears of their little brother and sister had caught the words.

"What's the secret?" cried Flossie excitedly. "Why did you want Bert to hush, Nan?"

"Because there isn't anything to tell," said

Nan truthfully enough. "But if I hear anything I'll tell you later," she added, and changed the subject.

"What were you two playing?" She looked toward the hole Flossie and Freddie had been making.

"We're digging a well," explained Freddie, "like on Uncle Daniel's farm."

"Some job!" said Bert, laughing.

"Don't laugh," said Flossie. "It's going to be a good well with water in it, maybe." She looked across the lawn to where Sam, the Negro gardener who worked for Mr. Bobbsey, was watering the flowers. "We asked Sam to squirt some water in our well hole to make it real. But he won't."

"We could squirt the water in the hole ourselves if he'd let us take the hose," said Freddie wistfully.

"But he won't let us have it!" exclaimed Flossie. "He says we'll squirt somebody and make a mess. But we wouldn't, would we, Freddie?"

"No," answered her twin loyally. Then he sighed. "I don't care. Come on, Flossie, we'll make a dry well."

"That'll be just as much fun," decided Flossie.

As the smaller twins walked slowly toward their "well," Bert fixed the hammock rope. Nan started for the house.

"If you hear anything about the secret let me know," Bert called.

"I will!" Nan promised.

The Bobbsey twins—both sets of them—had just come back from their summer vacation. It had been spent on the farm of their uncle Daniel Bobbsey at Meadow Brook. While there the twins had visited a county fair and their exciting adventures are told in THE BOBBSEY TWINS AT THE COUNTY FAIR.

But vacations always come to an end sooner or later, and this happened to the Bobbseys. They had returned to their home in Lakeport, on Lake Metoka.

"I wish we could have stayed longer," thought Bert, as he swung in the hammock. "It's too hot here, and it's not even the end of August! Jimminy! School opens in about three weeks!" He sighed a very deep sigh. "I wish it was three months!"

But still, as he thought it over and swung in the hammock, Bert could not help being glad that at least there were still three weeks more in which to have fun before school began.

"I'll start right now," Bert thought. He jumped out of the still swinging hammock and headed across the lawn. "I'll get Charlie Mason and we'll go swimming."

As he passed through the hall to pick up his swim trunks and tell Mrs. Bobbsey where he was going, Bert heard Nan singing a song

about work. She was helping her mother and
Dinah, Sam's wife, unpack suitcases after the
vacation at Uncle Daniel's farm.

"I won't be gone long," Bert called, and left
the house.

A short walk brought him to Charlie
Mason's house. Bert's friend was eager for a
swim, too, and in a few minutes both boys set
off for the lake. Charlie was Bert's age and size
with brown eyes and a good-natured grin.

Reaching the lake, Bert and Charlie
changed to their swim trunks in a boathouse,
then raced each other to the water.

Bert won, but Charlie challenged him to a
swimming race to a float anchored about fifty
feet offshore. This time Charlie climbed onto
the float first. Laughing and gasping for
breath, the two boys stretched out to dry off.

The slight rocking of the float and the hot
sun lulled them and soon both boys were dozing.

Suddenly Charlie yelled, "Yowee!" and
jumped to his feet. Startled, Bert looked up to
see what was wrong. A shower of cold water
struck his back and sent him scrambling to his
feet with a yelp.

"What—" he cried, then stopped short as he
spotted the town bully, Danny Rugg, swimming beside the float.

"Wouldn't you know!" Charlie said in disgust.

"This calls for a dunking, don't you think?" Bert asked his chum with a wink.

"Good idea. Let's make it right now. We're wet anyway."

"Wait, fellows!" Danny cried in alarm. "I was just kidding! If—if you promise not to dunk me I'll tell you an important secret."

Bert and Charlie looked skeptical, but Danny had already hauled himself aboard the float. He was a large boy, a little older than Bert. He liked to play mean tricks on children younger and smaller than himself.

"All right, let's hear this secret," Charlie growled, "before we decide to push you under."

A sly look came into Danny's eyes, and leaning forward, he whispered, "There's a mad bear loose just a few miles from here!"

"What!" Bert and Charlie exclaimed together, and Bert added, "Do you mean it has hydrophobia like dogs get sometimes?"

"Yes, and it's vicious—attacking people!"

"How do you know about this?" Charlie demanded.

Danny looked very secretive as he said, "Never mind how I found out. I heard it from someone who knows, but that's all I'll say."

"Now just where did you say this bear's supposed to be?" Bert probed.

"Well," Danny said, "maybe it was more than a few miles from here."

"All right, where?" Charlie demanded. "And tell us the truth!"

"Lake—Lake Melrose," the bully stammered.

Bert and Charlie exchanged glances and sighed with relief. As usual, Danny had made the story much worse than it really was. The nearest shore of Lake Melrose was about fifty miles away. It was joined with Lake Metoka, where the boys were swimming, by a small river.

"That mad bear—if there really is one— will be trapped long before it could come here, even if it wanted to!" Bert exclaimed.

"Sure," agreed Charlie. "Besides, I'll bet this is just another of Danny's wild tales."

"You wait!" cried Danny, angry that his story had not frightened the boys. "The mad bear will cause you trouble—bad trouble!"

With that, he dived off the float and struck out for shore.

Meanwhile, back at the Bobbsey home, Sam Johnson had continued sprinkling the flowers and grass. There had been a period of dry weather and the grass on the lawn was brown in many places. Sam was trying to bring it back to a fresh green color by using plenty of water.

Suddenly Freddie, who had been helping Flossie scoop dirt out of the well hole, dropped his shovel and started off.

"Where you going?" Flossie demanded.

Her twin did not answer, but Flossie needed only one look to tell her. Dinah, the Bobbseys' plump, good-natured cook, had called Sam to bring in a rug hanging on the line. Sam had dropped the hose, with the water still spurting from the nozzle, and Freddie had seen this.

Losing no time, he made a dash for the hose. This was a chance not to be missed! The water was turned on ready for him to use.

Freddie picked up the hose. A moment later he heard someone behind him. It was Flossie.

"Let me take it! I want to squirt!" she cried.

"No!" Freddie objected. "I got here first!"

He started to run, dragging the hose after him. The little boy headed for the place where he and Flossie had been digging.

"I'm going to fill our well with water!" Freddie shouted.

"I want to! I'm going to help!" declared Flossie, running after her brother. "I helped dig that hole, too, you know."

"This is man's work," Freddie cried boastfully. He might have reached the hole ahead of her if he had not had to drag the heavy hose. But it held him back, and Flossie caught up to him.

"Let me squirt it!" she demanded. She made a grab, trying to pull the nozzle from her brother's hands, but Freddie held on tightly.

All this happened while the water was spurting out in a heavy stream. As Flossie and Freddie struggled, one trying to hold the hose and the other trying to get it away, something had to happen and it did. The water, instead of spurting steadily in one place, showered all over the small twins.

"Oh, oh!" cried Flossie, as her dress became soaked. But she still held the nozzle, yanking and pulling on it to wrest it from her brother's grip.

"You did it!" cried Freddie. "Let go that nozzle."

"No, I want to fill the hole myself!" Flossie insisted.

She gave another pull on the hose. Suddenly the spray pointed at the house. In through an open window spurted the water! Excited shouts came from Dinah and Mrs. Bobbsey.

"Children! Children!" their mother exclaimed. "Be careful!"

"Land sakes, what you-all doing?" Dinah cried. "Goodness, you've drenched the chairs and carpet."

As she spoke, Dinah came to the window, her plump figure almost filling it. "Sam," she said, turning to her husband, who had rushed into the living room to see what the excitement was about, "why did you leave that water turned on when—"

But that was all Dinah could say, for suddenly a spurt of water from the hose hit her squarely in the face!

CHAPTER II

HINT OF TROUBLE

DISMAYED, Freddie and Flossie stared at the drenched Dinah. Freddie dropped the hose, and it twisted crazily.

"Freddie!" Mrs. Bobbsey exclaimed from the window. "Pick up that hose and turn it the other way! The water is ruining my lovely dahlias!"

Freddie had dropped the nozzle so that the water was splashing onto a flower bed near the house. Quickly he picked up the hose. A second later he heard Nan cry, "Oh, Freddie, you're aiming it right through the living-room window again! Stop!"

But the little boy was too bewildered to drop the hose or turn it off at the nozzle. There he stood, holding it so the spray streamed through the window.

"Land sakes!" exclaimed dripping wet Dinah. "This is worse than the flood Noah floated the ark in! Sam! Sam!" she cried. "Turn that water off!"

Her husband dashed outdoors and did this, but not before Flossie, Freddie, and Dinah had been well soaked, and water had sprayed most of the living room and kitchen.

The two six-year-olds went inside and helped wipe the water from furniture and rugs. Their mother made them promise that they would not touch the hose again. Soberly, the little twins went to their rooms to change into dry play suits. But Flossie's and Freddie's spirits could not stay low very long. Returning to the yard, they eagerly started once more with their well digging.

Soon they were busy carrying sand pails of water to the "well." But it seemed as if each time they made a trip, the water they had left in the hole had drained away.

"Oh dear!" sighed Flossie at last. "Our bee-yoo-ti-ful well has no bottom to it!" And this seemed to be true.

Finally the twins gave up, deciding to ask Uncle Daniel some day how he kept water in his well at the farm. As they walked back toward the house to see if lunch was ready, Freddie and Flossie saw Bert coming back from his swim with Charlie and Danny.

As Bert entered the house, he was still puzzling over Danny's odd story about a mad bear at Lake Melrose.

"What happened here?" he asked, when he saw Nan still busy with a cloth, wiping up the last of the water. "Something to do with the secret you were talking about, Sis?"

"Of course not!" answered Nan. She gave Bert a warning look.

But Mrs. Bobbsey had heard her son. "What's this about a secret?" she asked.

"Oh, Nan said Dad had one," replied Bert. "But—"

"What do you mean, Nan?" asked Mrs. Bobbsey.

"Well, I heard you and Dad talking about having to go away. I thought it was a secret, because Dad said not to mention anything about it for a while."

"Oh, *that!*" Mrs. Bobbsey laughed. "That isn't much of a secret."

Nan looked disappointed.

"I thought maybe we were going to have another vacation trip," she explained.

"I see," said Mrs. Bobbsey. Putting her hand on Nan's shoulder, she added, "It isn't wise, dear, to listen to half a conversation and then imagine the rest. It's all very simple. I know your father didn't intend it for a secret. Perhaps he'll tell you about it this noon."

"Couldn't you tell us?" asked Bert.

"I'd rather not. It's about Dad's lumber business," his mother answered.

"Oh, if it's about lumber I guess it isn't much of a secret," said Bert. Plainly disappointed, he walked out to the porch.

"Yes, it is, too!" Nan insisted in a whisper as she followed him. "I heard Dad say there might be a lot of trouble."

"Trouble!" exclaimed Bert. "I wonder why."

At lunch time, Mr. Bobbsey laughed when Mrs. Bobbsey told him what Nan had said about a secret.

"Well, in a way it is a secret, for I don't want everyone to know about it," he admitted. "But I'll tell you children."

Mr. Bobbsey said that there was a rumor of trouble in connection with some logs he had bought. He had purchased them from a man who had a tract of timber near Lake Melrose.

"Lake Melrose!" Bert exclaimed, sitting bolt upright in his chair.

"Why, yes," Mr. Bobbsey said, looking at his son curiously. "We've all been there. Is something wrong?"

"N-no," said Bert, deciding not to mention Danny's hints. "Uh, what sort of trouble is it?"

"I've heard that some men are threatening to take away the logs I've bought," went on Mr. Bobbsey. "I told your mother that I might have to make a trip to Melrose to see about it. I asked her not to mention this for the present, and I suppose that's why you imagined it was a secret, Nan. But I do expect to go to Lake Melrose next week."

"How long will you stay?" Mrs. Bobbsey asked.

"Oh, perhaps a week or two. Possibly three," he replied.

"Is there a hotel at the lake where you can stay?" asked Mrs. Bobbsey.

"No, I'll have to camp out, I guess."

"Oh! Camping out!" cried Freddie and Flossie, and Nan added, "Couldn't we camp with you, Dad?"

"Please take us!" begged the small twins. "School doesn't open for three weeks. We want to go camping. We want to go camping!"

"Children! Children! Please be quiet!" begged their mother. "Yes, what is it, Dinah?" she asked, as the cook appeared in the doorway of the dining room.

"Telephone call for Mr. Bobbsey," Dinah announced.

"It's probably the office," said the twins' father. He went to the hall and returned a few minutes later with a worried expression on his face.

"What is it, Dick?" Mrs. Bobbsey asked.

"The trouble has come sooner than I expected," he replied. "It seems that some men at Lake Melrose have already tried to take my lumber. I must go up there at once and see about it."

"Oh, take us! Take us with you!" begged Freddie and Flossie.

CHAPTER III

A NEW COOK

A SMILE replaced the worried frown on Mr. Bobbsey's face as he looked at the twins.

"Please, Dad, take us camping with you," begged Nan.

"It sure would be fun," said Bert softly. "Unless—"

"Unless what?" Nan prompted.

"Oh—oh, nothing," Bert replied.

"I could go fishing!" cried Freddie quickly.

"And swimming!" put in Flossie.

"You seem to have pretty good arguments, children," said Mr. Bobbsey. "What do you say, Mary?" he asked the twins' mother.

"Well, if you have to go," Mrs. Bobbsey said, "I think it would be a nice trip for all of us."

Flossie and Freddie looked at each other excitedly.

"Now, before I decide definitely," Mr. Bobbsey said, "I want to make one more phone call."

He returned to the hall for a few minutes. Meanwhile the twins talked in excited whispers of what they would do if they should go to Lake Melrose. All recalled the time they had had a wonderful picnic there. Mr. Bobbsey had showed them where a small river joined Lake Melrose with Lake Metoka, which was near the Bobbseys' home.

Rafts of logs could easily be floated from one lake to the other. Once they were in Lake Metoka they could be towed to Mr. Bobbsey's mill and sawed into boards.

Presently their father returned from the telephone. "Well," he said, "it's all settled. I've made arrangements to be away from the office, and—"

He paused and looked at the children with a twinkle in his eyes. "And you all will go with me!"

"Hurray!" cried Freddie.

"Goodie! Goodie!" shouted Flossie.

"So, Mary," Mr. Bobbsey went on, smiling, "if it isn't too much trouble for you to get ready to go on another trip, we'll do it."

"Oh, it won't really be any trouble," Mrs. Bobbsey said, smiling back. "We have only just started to unpack and Sam and Dinah can see that the house is closed. In fact, this might be a good time for them to visit Dinah's family in Virginia. That way they would have a vacation, too."

"Fine idea," Mr. Bobbsey said, and Mrs. Bobbsey went to the kitchen to tell Dinah.

"When can we go?" asked Freddie.

"Tomorrow," his father answered. "We'll go in the car, and take enough provisions to stay at least a couple of weeks."

"How will we camp?" Nan asked. "In a tent?"

"There's a bungalow on the lake," her father replied. "It isn't a very good one—more like a tumble-down shack than anything else—but I think it will do for the time we need it.

"Now," he added, "I must get back to the office right away. I'll leave it to you twins and your mother to get ready. We'll start for Lake Melrose as early as possible tomorrow morning."

"Hurray! Hurray!" shrieked Flossie and Freddie.

Mr. Bobbsey hurried off. The younger twins were bursting with excitement at the prospect of another vacation. Freddie stood on his head, and Flossie tried hard to do the same, but did not quite succeed.

"We'll help you get ready, Mother," Nan offered, as Mrs. Bobbsey returned to the living room. "Won't we, Bert?"

"Sure," Bert replied absently, wondering if he should tell his mother and Nan what Danny had said. But he could not quite make himself believe the story was true and he did not want to be laughed at—nor did he want to alarm the others unnecessarily.

"I'll need your help," Mrs. Bobbsey said.

She and the older twins went upstairs to begin packing the clothes the family would need for their camping trip. Food and other supplies could be taken care of by Dinah.

It was decided that Mrs. Bobbsey would pack for herself and the children's father. Nan would handle Flossie's and her own packing, and Bert, Freddie's and his clothes. The three separated to begin work.

A few minutes later, Bert and Nan heard their mother cry out as if in pain. They dashed up the hall and collided with Dinah, who had hurried up the stairs when she heard Mrs. Bobbsey's cry.

Untangling themselves, the three ran to Mrs. Bobbsey's side. She was bending over a suitcase, one hand clutching her right wrist.

"Mother, what's wrong?" Nan cried.

Mrs. Bobbsey managed a weak smile and held up her right hand. The palm had a long, ugly gash across it!

Instantly Bert dashed off and returned with the first aid kit. Nan helped her mother to a chair, then put antiseptic on the cut and began to bandage Mrs. Bobbsey's hand.

"How did it happen?" Nan asked, tearing off strips of adhesive.

Mrs. Bobbsey smiled ruefully. "It was very

careless of me, but I left my manicure scissors in the side pocket of my suitcase. Just now I reached in quickly to see if my brush was still packed. The point of the scissors caught my hand and slashed it."

"Gee, that's too bad, Mother," Bert said sympathetically. "Maybe we'd better not go to Lake Melrose after all."

Nan gave Bert a very puzzled look. This did not sound like him—giving up a camping trip!

"Oh, we won't call it off just for a little cut like this," Mrs. Bobbsey said.

"But that's not a little cut," Dinah insisted.

"It's pretty deep. I'm afraid that hand won't be much good to you for a while."

"But I'll have cooking and dishwashing to do on the camping trip," Mrs. Bobbsey protested.

Dinah smiled and said, "Now don't you-all worry yourself about that, Mis' Bobbsey. Sam and I can go to Virginny some other time. I'll just go right along with you and take care of everything."

Mrs. Bobbsey was about to protest further when Nan spoke up. "Dinah, there's no need for you to give up your vacation. *I'll* do the cooking!"

"Oh, oh!" cried Bert. "Now I *know* we should call off the trip!" He grinned at Nan.

"I can do it, Mother," Nan declared. "And Bert and Freddie and Flossie can be the dish washers! How about it, Bert?"

Her brother hesitated. Should he mention his worry about the rumor of the mad bear? But if it were not true, he would alarm his family needlessly and spoil their fun. Again, he decided to say nothing, but he promised himself that he would be on guard constantly while at the lake—just in case!

"Well?" Nan asked impatiently.

Bert smiled. "Sure. I don't mind washing dishes, but I think I'll buy a lot of paper plates!"

Nan made a face at him. Mrs. Bobbsey

agreed to the plan, and the older twins and Dinah finished the necessary packing.

Supper was prepared that evening by Nan under Dinah's supervision, and everyone— even Bert—agreed that she showed great promise as a cook.

Next morning the twins and Mrs. Bobbsey were ready and waiting for Mr. Bobbsey to bring the car from a near-by gas station. The day was bright and very warm.

"Here comes Daddy!" cried Freddie, as he caught sight of the approaching car.

Instantly there was a buzz of excitement, which quieted only after the baggage was stowed in the trunk and the family was seated in the car. Mr. and Mrs. Bobbsey were in front, the twins in the wide back seat. With the suit-cases were Freddie's toy fire engine and Flos-sie's favorite doll in a box.

As the Bobbseys drove away, Dinah and Sam stood at the curb waving good-by. Soon they, too, would be leaving on vacation. Snap, the dog, and Snoop, the cat, were also there to see the twins off. Snap barked and Snoop mewed.

Flossie and Freddie had wanted to take their pets with them. But their father had said the animals might get lost in the woods. So the smaller twins agreed to let Snoop and Snap re-main in Lakeport. Sam was to take the dog and cat to Mr. Bobbsey's lumberyard where the watchman would take care of them.

The Bobbseys had traveled several miles along the shore of Lake Metoka, when suddenly there was a loud noise like a shot.

"What's that?" Mr. Bobbsey cried sharply. "A tire blown out?"

He slowed the car and steered to the side of the road. But laughter from the twins in the rear seat soon made him realize that nothing serious had happened.

"It was my balloon," Freddie admitted. "It broke!"

"He blew it too big!" added Flossie. "Now I can't blow it! And we haven't any more balloons!"

"No," said Freddie sadly, looking at the limp shreds of his plaything. "Dad, would you stop at the next town and buy me one?"

"Ho! I don't believe I want to!" Mr. Bobbsey said, laughing, as he started the car again. "You gave me quite a scare. I thought a tire had blown out! No more balloons, Freddie, at least, not until we get to our camp."

"And then it's my turn to have one," insisted Flossie. "And now can't we eat?"

Dinah had packed a lunch for them to take in the car, and since it was near noon, Mr. Bobbsey stopped beneath some trees on a little used road. They got out, spread the red and blue picnic cloth, and opened boxes and baskets.

"It's lots of fun to eat this way," said Nan as she passed the sandwiches.

"Like a picnic," agreed Bert. "I'd rather eat this way any time than at a table."

"It saves washing dishes at any rate," observed Mrs. Bobbsey with a smile at Bert.

Flossie and Freddie finished their lunch first and asked if they might run around awhile. Mrs. Bobbsey agreed.

"Don't go far away," she cautioned them. "And stay out of the road."

Flossie and Freddie promised and ran among the trees. The others could hear them playing hide-and-seek. Then their voices grew fainter. Mrs. Bobbsey had just asked Bert and Nan to go after them when the twins saw Flossie come running down the road. Her hair was flying in the wind and her blue eyes were wide with fright.

"Oh, it's after Freddie!" she cried. "It's after Freddie!"

"What is?" her mother asked, worried. Above Flossie's cries could be heard the frightened shouts of the little boy. "Who's after Freddie?"

"A big sheep! And—and he's got horns!"

A moment later Freddie came into view, racing around a turn in the road. Behind the boy came a ram with large, curved horns.

"Daddy! Mother!" howled Freddie. "Catch him! Save me!"

CHAPTER IV

THE TUMBLE-DOWN COTTAGE

IT LOOKED as though the old sheep with the curved horns would catch up to Freddie any moment and butt him. No one could possibly get there in time to prevent it.

"Help, somebody!" cried the terrified little boy. "Help!"

"Throw something at the ram!" Nan cried as the huge sheep, head lowered, pounded after Freddie.

Instantly Bert's hand whipped into the glove compartment of the car and came out holding a heavy flashlight. He hurled it with all his might at the charging beast. It struck the ram's side with a thud.

Startled, the animal paused a moment. Then it pounded on.

"Run to the side, Freddie!" Mr. Bobbsey yelled. "Let him pass you!"

The little boy pivoted suddenly, almost losing his balance, and struck off to his right. Thundering past him not ten feet away, the ram plowed head on toward the rear of the car.

Crash! The ram hit the car, which lurched and shuddered, but the emergency brake held. Striking the bumper with such force made the ram actually rebound and he sat down hard in the road, legs sprawled in all directions! With eyes glazed from shock, he looked up at the Bobbseys and shook his head as if to say, "What hit me?"

In the meantime, Freddie, half sobbing, had run to his father, who snatched him up and put him on the car's front hood out of danger. Mrs. Bobbsey, forgetting her injured hand, swept up her small daughter and placed her beside Freddie.

"Will—will he come after me again?" whispered the little boy fearfully.

But the ram seemed to have had enough excitement for one day. Still shaking his head, he staggered to his feet and tottered off in the direction from which he had come.

Bert laughed. "That was some bump!" he said.

With a relieved smile, Mr. Bobbsey turned to Freddie. "Now, son," he asked, "just what did you do to make that ram chase you?"

"I—I only opened a gate to his field to pick some flowers," Freddie replied. "Wow, did he come after me!" He was feeling much better now that the danger had passed.

"You should never open a gate where there's

a strange animal, Freddie," Mrs. Bobbsey said. "One never knows—"

"Look!" cried Bert.

All of the Bobbseys looked up to see a grizzled man in overalls running down the road toward them. He stopped as he caught sight of the tottering ram.

"Did he make trouble for you?" the farmer called. "I don't know how the ram got out of his pasture. I keep him penned in all the time because he's an ugly one and even goes for me sometimes."

"I'm afraid my little boy let him out," Mr. Bobbsey spoke up. "He didn't know the ram was ugly. But I don't think he'll give you any trouble now. The old fellow ran full tilt into the rear bumper of our car!"

"And he bounced!" Flossie added.

"Ha! Serves him right," the farmer said, laughing. "Well, I'm glad no one was hurt." Turning to the ram, he said, "Get along now, Ebeneezer!" And meekly the ram allowed himself to be driven back to the pasture.

Mr. Bobbsey inspected the rear bumper. It was dented and scratched from the ram's horns, but the damage could be repaired easily. Then Mrs. Bobbsey told the twins to get back into the car.

Soon they were on their way again. Freddie and Flossie played a game with the license plates they spotted on cars along the highway.

Nan busied herself with pencil and paper, planning the family's menus for the next week.

Only Bert sat quietly, lost in thought. The story Danny had told about the mad bear was still worrying him. Bert's common sense told him that Danny had probably made up the tale on the spur of the moment to escape being dunked. But on the other hand, suppose it were true!

Bert's thoughts were interrupted when Nan leaned over and whispered in his ear, "What's wrong, Bert? You've been acting strangely ever since Dad mentioned this trip. Don't you want to go camping?"

Deciding to take Nan into his confidence, Bert said in a low voice, "It's like this, Nan—"

Suddenly Bert stopped talking. There was a sharp, hissing sound outside the car.

"Ooh!" exclaimed Flossie. "We've run over a snake! I can hear him hissing!"

Mr. and Mrs. Bobbsey and the older twins laughed, but Freddie looked rather puzzled. This was no snake. It was just a flat tire!

Mr. Bobbsey was disgusted. "I thought I bought puncture-proof tires," he said. "That garage man must have given me the wrong kind."

Bert climbed out with his father to change the tire and Freddie volunteered to help.

"Suppose the girls and I walk over to that farmhouse up ahead while you're busy with the tire," Mrs. Bobbsey suggested. "I'm very thirsty and I'm sure we can get some cool water there."

"Fine," Mr. Bobbsey agreed. "The boys and I will come for you when we finish."

A short walk brought Nan, Flossie, and their mother to the pleasant, rambling farmhouse. It looked very welcoming and cool beneath towering old oak trees.

A sweet-faced, middle-aged woman in jeans and blouse was working in the garden at the back of the house. When the Bobbseys approached, she looked up and smiled.

"Hello," Mrs. Bobbsey said, and introduced herself and her daughters. Then she explained about the flat tire.

"That's too bad," said the farm woman, adding that her name was Mrs. Sill.

"Like in *window?*" Flossie asked.

Mrs. Sill nodded and laughed. "Yes, dear, exactly like in *window!* Now, I'm sure you are all thirsty."

She led the Bobbseys into a bright, cheery kitchen with gingham curtains and pine paneling. And to Nan's delight, there was a huge old-fashioned fireplace in one corner with rocking chairs beside the hearth.

"Is this a Dutch oven?" Nan asked, pointing to a copper door set in one side of the fireplace.

"Indeed it is," was the reply.

Mrs. Sill opened the copper door and, on both shelves of the oven, pans of sugar cookies were baking. How delicious they smelled!

"They're done to a turn," Mrs. Sill said. "Just in time for my visitors."

In a few minutes, Nan, Flossie, and Mrs. Bobbsey were seated at a round table enjoying tall glasses of cool, fresh milk and the large, oval sugar cookies—still warm from the oven. When Mr. Bobbsey and the boys appeared at the kitchen door, they were invited in, too. After washing up, they joined the little party.

His mouth full of cookies, Freddie looked wonderingly at Mrs. Sill. After swallowing, he said, "Boy, can you bake cookies, Mrs. Sill!"

Suddenly Freddie sniffed. "Are some cookies burning? I'll get my little fire engine out of the car."

Mrs. Sill dashed to the oven. "Thank you, little man. One more minute and the cookies would have needed a fire engine!" She pulled out the well-browned, crisp cookies.

With many thanks to the kindly Mrs. Sill, the Bobbseys returned to the car and continued on their way. About three o'clock they spotted Lake Melrose from the top of a hill. After driving several miles along the wooded shoreline, they turned onto a narrow dirt road.

"This sure isn't much of a road," Bert said as the car gave a tremendous bounce.

"No," his father replied, "but it's very short and leads directly to the bungalow. Ah, there's the place now."

Through a deeply shadowed glen, the Bobbseys caught sight of a brown, weathered cottage
nestled among tall pines.

"Oh, it's lovely!" Nan cried.

"But it's in quite a run-down condition, I'm
afraid," her father replied.

"No matter what condition it's in," said Mrs.
Bobbsey, "it will be much cooler here than in
Lakeport."

When they stopped in front of the bungalow,
Flossie and Freddie were the first ones out of
the car. They dashed up the rickety front steps
with Nan and Bert behind them. The four children peered between slats in the window shutters to see what the inside of their temporary
home was like.

"I see bunks in a bedroom!" cried Freddie.

Mr. Bobbsey opened the front door and
everyone walked inside. How dusty the place
looked! Tiny motes danced in the broad beam
of sunlight from the open door and settled
lightly on the table and chairs in the main
room.

The children ran to unbar the shutters and
open the doors to the kitchen and bedrooms.
While Bert helped his father unload the car,
Nan, Flossie, and Freddie scurried about with
brooms and dustcloths. Within an hour the
Bobbsey family was settled in its vacation cottage.

"What wonderful assistants you are!" Mrs.

Bobbsey said delightedly. "But I feel so helpless with this bandaged hand."

"You're the supervisor, Mother," Nan replied with a smile.

She asked Mrs. Bobbsey to direct the work of cleaning the kitchen and putting away the supplies they had brought. Bert was put in charge of the water supply. In back of the house was a spring with clear, ice-cold water bubbling over rocks.

Coming back from a trip to the spring, Bert called to his father, who was setting out the porch furniture.

"Where's your lumber, Dad?"

"About fifty feet down the shore. Shall we go and look it over?"

"I'll be right with you," Bert replied. He ran the rest of the way to the kitchen with two buckets of water, then returned.

Mr. Bobbsey and Bert walked along the sandy shore and soon spotted the lumber stacked in a huge pile. Two rough-looking men dressed in jeans and high laced boots were standing beside it.

"Hello!" Mr. Bobbsey called, walking toward them. "What can I do for you?"

"Not a thing, mister," the taller man growled. "We're just watching over our lumber!"

"*Your* lumber!" Bert exclaimed, then looked at his father in amazement.

CHAPTER V

A FUNNY FISH

MR. BOBBSEY was just as surprised as Bert at the words of the lumberman. Could these men be part of the group who had threatened to take his logs?

Turning to the taller man who had spoken to them, he said, "I'm afraid there's been a mistake. I believe these are logs I bought and I'm up here to arrange having them rafted and shipped to my lumberyard in Lakeport."

The two woodsmen exchanged glances, then the taller one took a few steps toward Bert and his father. His bushy eyebrows narrowed over his small glittering eyes.

"Those logs aren't going anywhere, mister. Not until we're paid. We got a claim on 'em. Besides, we've got four more buddies across the lake who'll help us see that the logs stay right here. Understand?"

"No, I don't," Mr. Bobbsey said evenly. "Perhaps you had better explain just what claim this is you're talking about."

"Our claim for wages that are due us for cutting this timber!" the shorter, heavy-set lumberman growled.

"Right!" the other one snapped. "Say, what's your name, mister?"

"Bobbsey. Richard Bobbsey."

"That's it! That's the name of the man who owes us our wages!" the tall man shouted. "Look, Bobbsey, we've earned that money and we want it right now."

Bert glanced up at his fine-looking father. Mr. Bobbsey seemed very calm. He talked quietly to the men a few moments, saying he was sure the whole mix-up could be straightened out. Then he explained that he had purchased the trees already cut from a Mr. Kling who had acted as agent for a lumbering concern.

The men seemed puzzled by his words, and still suspicious. They identified themselves as Mark Lanyard and Chuck Grimes and said a man named Wadell had hired them to cut down the timber. Mr. Wadell had told them he was the agent for a Mr. Bobbsey who would pay them for the work.

"Do you know where we could find this Mr. Wadell?" Mr. Bobbsey asked.

"Yeah, sure," Grimes, the tall lumberman, replied. "He lives about forty miles from here. Why?"

"I suggest you bring this man here to talk

with me," Mr. Bobbsey said. "I've never heard of him and he certainly had no authority to use my name in any business dealings."

Chuck Grimes pointed his finger at Bert's father and cried, "Oh, no, you don't! If we leave to go get Wadell, how do we know you won't ship the timber off while we're gone?"

Bert knew his father was angry, but all Mr. Bobbsey said was, "You have my word. That lumber will still be here when you get back. I want to straighten this out as much as you do."

Grimes and Lanyard scuffled their feet in the sand and shrugged. Evidently this was not enough to convince them.

"All right," Mr. Bobbsey said, still in a calm manner. "It will take me several days to hire men and have these logs rafted. I couldn't possibly get them shipped before you return. Besides, my family is with me on a camping vacation and we plan to be here for about two weeks."

By this time Bert was furious with the lumbermen for being so distrustful of his father. He was just about to make a sharp remark, when Lanyard said:

"Okay. I guess that makes sense. But remember, no tricks. This lumber had better be here when we get back or there'll be trouble! I'm still not convinced this isn't a trick to cheat us out of our wages!"

Before Mr. Bobbsey could retort, Grimes

and Lanyard turned and stalked off down the beach. For a moment after they had gone, Bert was so angry he could not speak. Finally he managed to choke out, "Well, of all the—"

"Take it easy, son," Mr. Bobbsey said, putting a hand on Bert's shoulder. "I know how you feel, and believe me, I'm angry too. But we must remember that these men have evidently been cheated out of their wages by someone, and they need the money. I'm sure this will be straightened out when Mr. Wadell arrives."

On the way back to the cabin Bert suddenly realized that he had forgotten all about the possibility of there being a mad bear in the area. He chided himself for not having been on guard. He would have to tell Nan at the first opportunity and perhaps she could help him decide whether or not to warn the rest of the family.

When he and his father entered the kitchen, Nan was preparing supper for the family. Mrs. Bobbsey was a bit worried when she learned of the encounter with the lunbermen, but the twins' father assured her that everything would be all right.

"At least," he said, "now I know why the men have been threatening to take the logs."

Freddie and Flossie set the table for supper and Bert helped Nan mash the potatoes. He insisted on sampling everything, looking very doubtful as he tasted the roast and peas. But finally he grinned at Nan and said, "I guess the Bobbseys will eat after all!"

Nan knew this was high praise and although she pretended to be angry, she was very pleased. Her brother's good opinion was important to her.

After the evening meal, Freddie and Flossie offered to build a bonfire so the whole family could enjoy a marshmallow roast on the beach. Everyone was enthusiastic, and soon, with Bert's help, a blaze was started.

While the firelight flickered against the darkening sky and danced on the water of the lake, the Bobbseys sang songs and told stories—between bites of the luscious marshmallows.

When Flossie and Freddie began to yawn and rub their eyes sleepily, Mrs. Bobbsey took them back to the cabin and soon they were calling good night to each other from their rooms.

When Mrs. Bobbsey returned to the beach, she said, "I think perhaps the rest of us should go to bed now, too. It's been a busy day."

Mr. Bobbsey agreed, but Bert asked if he and Nan might stay a little while longer to make sure the fire was out. His parents consented, and as soon as the twins were alone, Bert said:

"Nan, I've been wanting to talk to you about something I heard yesterday. It's been worrying me ever since. Charlie and I went swimming and Danny Rugg showed up. He said—"

'The Bobbseys sang songs and toasted marshmallows

His voice was suddenly drowned out. A shrill scream from the direction of the cabin slashed through the stillness!

"That was Flossie!" Nan cried, and instantly she and Bert scrambled to their feet and dashed for the bungalow.

The scene inside was both strange and laughable. Mrs. Bobbsey, in robe and slippers, held a lighted kerosene lantern in the doorway of Flossie and Nan's room. In the fluttering glow of the light Mr. Bobbsey, also in robe and slippers, was jumping madly about, waving a broom!

"What happened?" Bert yelled over the screams of Flossie, who was hiding behind her mother, and the thumping of overturned furniture.

"It's a mouse-bird!" Flossie cried. "He pulled my hair."

"A what?" Nan asked.

"A bat," said her mother.

Suddenly Mr. Bobbsey yelled, "Bert! Run outside and unhook the screen from this window. I'm going to shoo the bat out that way."

Bert dashed to the front door, sprang down the steps and raced to the window. Ten seconds later he had the screen off and *whoosh!* He ducked just as a dark shadow swooped past his face and into the night!

Within ten minutes, the house was peaceful again. Flossie was back in her bunk bed, Bert had replaced the screen, and Nan was getting ready for bed.

Suddenly Bert said to his mother, "Where was Freddie all this time?"

With a startled look on her face, Mrs. Bobbsey went to the door of Bert and Freddie's room and peeped inside. Freddie was in his bunk sound asleep. He had slept through it all!

What a teasing he was given the next morning at breakfast when the incident of the bat was discussed. Blushing and grinning, Freddie said he was going to go fishing and catch the biggest fish in the lake to make up for being such a sleepyhead!

His father gave him permission to use the small rowboat if he would not go far from shore. The lake was shallow for some distance out and Freddie could swim fairly well.

Bert and Mr. Bobbsey, keeping one eye on Freddie, walked toward the pile of logs to figure the number of rafts that would be required to float them to the mill. Nan was baking a chocolate pie, while Flossie washed her doll's clothes in the lake. Mrs. Bobbsey was watching the small twins from the porch.

The morning was clear and very quiet until Flossie suddenly called from the dock, "Mother! Daddy! Come quick! A big fish is towing Freddie out into the middle of the lake!"

CHAPTER VI

NAN SHARES A SECRET

"WHAT does Flossie mean?" Mrs. Bobbsey cried in alarm, hurrying to the lake front with Nan close behind her.

Flossie's blue eyes were wide with fright as she gasped out, "A fish—Freddie caught a fish and it's swimming away with him and the boat!"

By this time Mr. Bobbsey and Bert had reached the water too. All of them stared out over the lake where Freddie crouched in the bow of the rowboat. He held a fishpole in his chubby hands. The little boat was whisked this way and that through the water, as though some huge fish had hold of the hook.

"Freddie! Let go!" Mr. Bobbsey shouted.

But Freddie either did not hear him or did not want to lose his prize fish, for he still held the rod. As Mr. Bobbsey ran toward another boat to go rescue his son, whatever was pulling

Freddie suddenly veered sharply to the right. His family gasped as the little boy toppled over. The boat tipped wildly, almost capsizing!

"Freddie!" cried Mr. Bobbsey. "Let go of the pole quickly—before you're pulled in!"

But by now the little craft had righted itself and Freddie was back on his feet, grimly clutching the pole.

"Freddie! Freddie! Let go!" called his mother.

"I — don't — want to — lose — my — fish!" shouted Freddie, his words coming in gasps, for it was hard work to talk and keep hold of the pole.

Mr. Bobbsey rowed out with quick, strong strokes and was soon at his son's side.

"What have you caught, Freddie?" he cried, as his boat rubbed alongside. "Here, let me get hold of your line!"

"No, I want to pull it in myself!" insisted Freddie.

The little boy tried again to lift the pole high enough to bring up whatever was fast to the end of the line, for he did not have a reel on which the line could be wound in. But as he raised the pole it bent nearly double.

"Look out, Freddie, or it will break!"

"That's what I'm 'fraid of," Freddie said. "Else I could pull this fish in myself."

"Well, you certainly have something very

lively on your hook," remarked Mr. Bobbsey. The line was still swishing back and forth in the water, but whatever was on the hook could not be seen. "Hold still a minute and I'll get hold of the line and pull it in. The line won't break as quickly as the pole will."

Mr. Bobbsey reached over and caught hold of Freddie's line. As he pulled, the thing beneath the water tried hard to swim away, but Mr. Bobbsey had a firm hold and kept on drawing in.

One last heave and out of the water came a long, snakelike head and a huge, round brown body that twisted and lunged in the air.

Freddie had caught a snapping turtle!

Almost hypnotized, Freddie stared into the wicked-looking beady eyes.

"You don't want this, Freddie. It isn't a fish at all," said Mr. Bobbsey.

"Yes, I do want it!" cried Freddie. "I'm going to make a pen for it and keep it!"

But the turtle solved the problem himself. With a hard snap of his jaws he cut the line close to where it entered his mouth and dropped back into the water with a loud splash.

"There he goes!" cried Flossie.

"Oh, he's gone—my nice big turtle!" sighed Freddie, a look of disappointment on his face.

The other Bobbseys heaved sighs of relief, and Bert began to chuckle. The more he thought about the expression on his brother's face, the harder he laughed. Soon everyone was roaring, and even Freddie had to grin at his own mistake about the big fish. When he docked his boat, he vowed that the next one would not get away!

After lunch the four twins formed a clean-up crew, and within an hour the old bungalow was thoroughly scrubbed and shining.

"How about a swim?" Bert suggested.

A mad scramble followed to see who could don his swimsuit first and dash to the shore. Within five minutes the four children were splashing happily along the beach.

"Let's turn the boat upside down and you and I dive off it," Bert called to Nan.

"Okay," she agreed, "but we'll have to pull it up on shore afterwards to dry."

Swimming hard, she and Bert towed the boat out to a point where the water was deep enough for diving, and scrambled aboard.

"Last one off has to sweep the kitchen tonight!" Nan cried and did a perfect racing dive off her end of the craft.

Bert was caught off guard. The boat veered almost straight upward as Nan's weight destroyed the balance. Back he went, head over heels into the water and came up spluttering and coughing.

"Oh! You!" he gasped, heading toward Nan, who was treading water and giggling. "Now you're in for it!"

"You'll have to catch me first!" his sister called and began swimming with long, fast strokes toward the shore.

Nan reached shallow water and splashed toward the sandy beach, but at the last minute she stumbled. In a flash Bert caught her ankle and pulled her back into deeper water.

This time Nan came up spluttering and managed to gasp, "Okay, you win! I'm sorry."

Resting for a moment to get their breath, brother and sister swam back for the boat and towed it to the beach where the younger twins helped turn it over to dry off.

While Flossie and Freddie were practicing shallow dives off the end of the dock, Bert finally got a chance to whisper his secret to Nan. At first she was terrified at the idea of a mad bear on the loose near by. Then when Bert reminded her that Danny had refused to tell where he had heard the story, she began to wonder if the bully perhaps had made up the whole thing.

"Danny often tells wild stories," she said thoughtfully.

"That's what makes me wonder if he thought this one up on the spur of the moment to keep from being dunked by Charlie and me," Bert said. "But just suppose—"

"Yes, I know what you're thinking. Bert, shouldn't we tell Mother and Dad? Flossie and Freddie might wander off and it would be just horrible if something should happen."

Bert picked up a handful of sand and let it trickle through his fingers as he stared across the sun-speckled water.

"On the other hand," he said slowly, "I'd hate to spoil our whole vacation if it's just a wild story. Freddie and Flossie would be scared to go anywhere and Mother and Dad would be so worried they might even leave before Dad's lumber is taken care of."

Nan nodded soberly and for several moments

the twins were silent. At last Bert spoke up.

"Tell you what. Suppose you and I keep a close watch on Freddie and Flossie—to make sure they stay near the cabin, and within calling distance of either Mother or Dad."

Nan smiled. "That'll be some job, knowing the twins. But we'll do it. Maybe we can think up some other safeguards too. Let's really concentrate on it. Okay?"

"Right." Bert grinned. "And now, chief cook and bottle washer, may I remind you that it's time to start supper?"

"Cook, yes," Nan said with a twinkle in her eye. "But any bottles I leave to you!"

Mr. Bobbsey was rather silent during dinner that evening, and Bert knew he was worried because the lumbermen had not returned with Mr. Wadell. Just before bedtime, Bert had a chance to talk with his father alone.

"Dad," he said, "do you think Grimes and Lanyard really intend to bring back that man who they said hired them?"

Mr. Bobbsey seemed startled by the question. "Possibly not," he said. "But they may merely have been delayed. Perhaps Mr. Wadell couldn't get away immediately. Or they may have settled their claim and cleared up the mistake already."

Bert nodded, but secretly he still had a strange feeling that there would be more trouble from the surly lumbermen.

Next morning when Bert was on "kitchen detail," as he called the dishwashing chore, he told Nan of his idea for another safeguard against the mad bear.

"What do you say we build a bear trap out of some of the odd-size logs Dad doesn't plan to have shipped to his mill?"

Nan thought this over, then said, "Won't it be too hard?"

"No," Bert replied. "Nothing to it. I saw a picture of how to make one in an old book in Dad's library."

Mr. Bobbsey had left earlier to drive to a farm about five miles away for fresh eggs and milk. He also planned to contact some lumbermen to raft his logs. The older twins told their mother where they would be and started for the lumber pile.

"Let's ask Freddie and Flossie to help with some of the smaller logs," Nan suggested. "In that way we can keep an eye on them and still build the trap."

Bert thought his sister's idea a good one, and during the rest of the morning the four children gathered and placed the lumber according to Bert's instructions. At one point, Freddie asked Flossie what they were building.

"Why, a play house, I guess," Flossie replied, and Bert winked at Nan. They knew the small twins would worry if they learned the real purpose of the penlike structure.

After a quick lunch of milk, sandwiches, and fruit, the children returned to work. When the trap was almost finished, Bert lashed some small sticks together with twine to form a door. He tied them to the top of a large opening in the front. Then, stepping inside the pen, he looked about, trying to figure out just how this door should be arranged. He knew it was supposed to swing shut when anything touched the bait which would be placed in the middle of the pen.

Suddenly he heard a grating sound, then a loud *crack!* In terror he started for the opening, yelling to Nan and the younger twins to run.

Nan had grabbed her little brother and sister at the first grating sound and pulled them away from the trap. But Bert was caught inside.

With a rumble and crash the logs toppled in on each other and on Bert!

CHAPTER VII

THE MISSING PIE

"BERT!" Nan cried, tears streaming down her face. "Oh, Bert, are you hurt?"

A low moan came from somewhere inside the pile of tumbled logs. Then, to Nan's relief, she heard Bert say:

"I—I'm okay, I think. No bones broken, but I'm trapped in here. I can't move. The logs are all crisscrossed around me like jackstraws."

"Don't try to move, Bert," Nan called. Then turning to Flossie, she said, "Run to the cabin and get Mother. Hurry!"

The little girl dashed away. Frantically Nan and Freddie tackled the tangled mass of logs and Nan tried to comfort her brother. "If only Dad were here!" she thought.

In a few minutes Flossie returned with Mrs. Bobbsey. Not stopping to ask how the accident had occurred, she began pulling off some of the larger logs at the top, ignoring the pain from her cut hand.

Flossie sprang to help, but Mrs. Bobbsey told

the younger twins kindly that she and Nan had
better do it alone. "We must be very careful,
for some of these logs are probably holding up
the very ones which might fall and crush Bert."

Flossie and Freddie were disappointed, but
they realized that their mother was right. So
they waited until a log was removed from the
pile, then rolled it out of the way to make room
for others.

Very cautiously, Mrs. Bobbsey and Nan
tested each log before removing it. The task
was a long, tedious one and several times Bert
asked them please to hurry.

Nan and her mother exchanged glances.
Both were becoming tired, and it seemed im-
possible that they could ever manage to free
Bert without help. But they would not give up.

Suddenly there was a crackling in the brush
near by. In terror, Nan thought, "Could this
be the mad bear?"

But a moment later she was relieved when a
friendly voice called, "Hello!" A tall, well-
built farm boy stepped from the brush and
approached the Bobbseys. He was deeply
tanned and wore dungarees and a plaid shirt.

With a puzzled look he glanced at the tumbled logs and then at Mrs. Bobbsey. "What happened?" he asked.

Quickly Mrs. Bobbsey explained. Even before she had finished speaking, the lad began
pulling off some of the larger logs. Nan no-

ticed that he, too, was very careful to test each one first to be sure it could be removed without danger to Bert.

As he worked with Nan and her mother, the youth identified himself as William Stoddard. He said he lived on his father's farm about two miles away.

Keeping steadily at the job, the three finally managed to pull the remaining logs off Bert. At last he was free!

Bert heaved a sigh of relief and climbed gingerly to his feet. He was covered with dirt and bits of bark. One foot had been pinched between two heavy logs, and his right arm was bruised, but otherwise, he seemed all right.

"Boy, was I lucky!" he exclaimed.

"You certainly were," his mother replied seriously. "Please, Bert, no more playing with such heavy logs. You might have been badly injured."

Then she introduced William Stoddard and explained that without his help, Bert might still be imprisoned among the fallen logs.

"Call me Bill," the boy said, smiling. "Well, I'll have to get back to the farm. Glad you weren't hurt, Bert."

Suddenly Bert had an idea. "I'll walk part way with you," he said. "The exercise will help me get rid of some of the stiffness."

As Bert and the farm boy struck off through the woods, Nan, Mrs. Bobbsey, and the small twins walked slowly back to the cabin. How happy they were that Bert was safe and free again!

Meanwhile Bert and Bill were discussing bear traps. Bert had told his new friend that the pile of logs had really been intended to catch a bear.

"But why would you want to build a trap?" Bill asked, looking at Bert with a puzzled expression. "There aren't any bears around here."

"Are you sure?" Bert asked.

"Well, pretty sure," the youth replied. "Why?"

"Oh—oh, nothing much. I just heard a rumor that there was a mad bear in this area. Probably nothing to it."

"Well, now that you mention it," said Bill, "I did hear that a mean bear got loose from a circus. But I thought he'd been caught."

Bert thanked Bill Stoddard for helping to free him, then said good-by. When he reached the cabin, Bert drew Nan aside and told her what Bill had said.

Nan was relieved to learn that at least part of Danny's story might be false. But the twins agreed that it would be wise to keep a sharp look-out at all times, for Danny had told the story as if the bear were still at large.

"And he just might be," thought Bert.

Mr. Bobbsey returned home before supper with fresh eggs and other supplies. He reported that he had hired four lumbermen to raft his logs. They were to start work within the week.

"But we won't have to leave when the men come, will we?" Flossie asked anxiously. She had come to love the cabin by the lake and wished that her family might stay here a long time.

Mr. Bobbsey smiled. "Oh, no. It will take the men a couple of days just to make the rafts. Then they must stack them with the logs. And of course I can't leave until the work is completed. So we will all be able to enjoy quite a lot more camping, Flossie."

"Goodie," she said and hugged her father.

Bert asked his dad if he had heard any news about Grimes and Lanyard, the surly lumbermen who had threatened to take Mr. Bobbsey's logs. The answer was no. The twins' father said he was worried about it. He hoped that their not returning meant they had succeeded in settling their claim. But there was no assurance of this.

Next day the four children arose early and enjoyed a quick swim in the lake before breakfast. Later Flossie and Freddie went out in one of the small boats with their father. They promised to bring back a fat trout for dinner.

Bert and Nan took baskets and walked to a clearing in the woods to gather wild blackberries. Nan had just discovered a large patch of bushes when something slithered over her shoe. Her startled cry brought Bert on the run.

"It's a snake!" Nan cried. "Oh, kill it, Bert!"

Her brother grabbed a large stick and crept toward the snake which had disappeared behind a rock. Then, to Nan's shocked surprise, he dropped the stick and laughed.

"Oh, Nan," he said, "it's just a harmless little garter snake."

His sister went to look at the coiled snake, then grinned ruefully. "You're right. When it crawled over my foot, I was so scared I didn't notice what it was."

"He's about ten times as scared as you are," Bert pointed out. "All he wants to do is get away, and look! There he goes."

By the time Nan had glanced down again, the snake was gone. "Whew!" she breathed. "I'm glad it wasn't a poisonous one."

"There aren't many kinds of poisonous snakes around here," Bert replied.

Now that she had time to think about this, Nan realized her brother was right. And she knew that snakes are too valuable to be destroyed unless they are endangering human life. By eating rats, mice, and insects which might otherwise destroy the farmers' crops, they prove to be very valuable.

"Thanks for coming to my rescue, just the same," Nan said, as the twins started picking berries.

When they returned to the cabin some time

later, their baskets were brimming with juicy blackberries. Nan and Bert found Freddie in the kitchen. He was proudly displaying three large fish which he, Flossie, and Mr. Bobbsey had caught.

"We all had good luck," the little girl said.

That night the Bobbseys enjoyed a fish fry over a campfire on the beach. For dessert, there were fresh blackberries and thick cream. Later, when the sun had set, and a sliver of moonlight was rippling across the lake, Mr. Bobbsey said:

"I think we'll have good weather tomorrow. How would you all like to go on a long hike through the woods? We could carry a picnic lunch with us."

His suggestion was met by shouts of glee from the small twins. Bert and Nan exchanged glances, wondering what they would do if they should come face to face with the mad bear.

Mrs. Bobbsey felt that the trip would be fun for all of them. "And there are enough blackberries left for a little pie for each of us," she added. "My hand is well enough now for me to help Nan prepare them."

The following morning the Bobbsey family was bustling about early. Soon the tantalizing aroma of sizzling bacon was mixed with that of baking pies. When the pies were taken from the oven, they were wrapped in foil and placed in the Bobbseys' picnic baskets, along with plenty of sandwiches, fruit, and potato salad. Also, Nan had filled a large thermos with milk and a smaller one with tea for her parents.

By nine o'clock they were on their way. The path they chose wound in and out among the trees, but it never led the hikers far from the sparkling lake. Flossie and Freddie, pretending they were advance scouts for an exploring party, skipped ahead.

"We'd better speed up a little," Bert whispered to his twin. "We don't want to lose sight of them in case—"

He did not need to finish the sentence. Nan understood that he was worried about the possibility of a mad bear roaming the area. So the older twins walked near their little brother and sister until the whole family stopped in a lovely glen for lunch.

As usual, Flossie and Freddie finished first, and reached for their little pies.

"Oh!" Flossie exclaimed. "My pie is gone! Freddie, did you take it?"

"No."

"Then where did it go?"

No one could explain the strange disappearance. Suddenly Bert and Nan looked at each other, the same frightening thought occurring to both of them. Perhaps some wild animal who liked sweet things had crept up behind Flossie and taken the pie. Could it have been a bear?

CHAPTER VIII

FREDDIE BAILS OUT

"WHY are you children looking at each other?" Mrs. Bobbsey asked Bert and Nan. "Are you teasing your little sister by hiding her pie?"

"I didn't," said Nan.

"Me either," chimed in Bert.

"It would have been a good trick, though." Freddie giggled.

Suddenly Nan cried out, "Oh, Mother, I see the pie!"

"Where?" everyone asked at once.

"Flossie's sitting on it."

"Goodness, no!" Mrs. Bobbsey exclaimed, glancing at her younger daughter.

Flossie was now seated on the grass, her knees tucked up under her chin. She had rolled the log away as it was too uncomfortable to sit on. And peeking out from under her skirt was an edge of the pie crust.

When Flossie realized this she jumped up. "Who put the pie under me?" she wailed, daubing at the stains on her dress. "Did you, Freddie?"

"NO!"

This made everybody laugh, and Mrs. Bobbsey said she was sure nobody had done it. "When you got up to roll the log away you accidentally sat down on the pie."

"Oh dear, it's ruined," Flossie said as she picked up the dessert, which now looked extra flat, with dark juice oozing all around the edges.

"It's not ruined for me," Freddie piped up. "I'll eat it for you, Flossie."

Hearing this, his twin poked a cautious finger in the pie and tasted it. "Um, it's good—it doesn't taste sat-on," she exclaimed. "Anybody want some?"

Flossie didn't wait for an answer. She scooped up bits of broken crust and bright berries and stuffed them in her mouth.

"For goodness sakes, Flossie," Mrs. Bobbsey said. "Look at you now!"

Flossie's mouth and cheeks, too, were covered with berry stain. Mrs. Bobbsey led the little girl to a near-by brook to wash. By this time everyone had finished eating their sandwiches and fruit, and Nan packed the remaining food in a basket.

"All set for more adventures?" Mr. Bobbsey asked when the picnic had been cleared away.

"Yippee!" Freddie exclaimed. "Let's go!"

The four Bobbseys scampered on ahead of their parents, exploring every little dell and glen along the way.

"Freddie's like a hunting dog," Mr. Bobbsey said, chuckling. "He covers more ground than a setter."

"He seems to be looking for something," Mrs. Bobbsey remarked. Then she called out, "What are you hunting for, Freddie?"

"It's a secret," came the reply. "But I'll tell you when I find it."

"Find what?" Bert asked, running over to where his younger brother was glancing up into a tree. Freddie pulled Bert's head down alongside his own and whispered into his ear.

"Great!" was all that Bert said.

"Tell us the secret, too," demanded Nan and Flossie.

But the boys would not do this. "When we find it, you'll have fun, too," Bert told his sisters with a wink.

He had hardly said this when Freddie shouted, "I see one!"

The girls fully expected to see a squirrel or rabbit dash out of the woods, but their brother was pointing at a limb sticking straight out from a near-by tree.

"That's the secret!" Freddie shouted.

"What's so secret about a tree branch?" Flossie wanted to know.

"So we can make a swing," Freddie said.

"But we haven't any rope," Nan said.

"We'll make a Robin Hood rope," Bert suggested.

"Oh, I know," Nan said. "A vine rope."

"Sure, there are lots of vines around," Bert said. "Come on, everybody. Let's find them."

Mr. and Mrs. Bobbsey joined in the search for vines, and soon a whole pile of them lay on the ground near the tree. Quickly Bert and Nan braided them into a stout rope.

"There, that's long enough," Bert said, holding up the strand he and his sister had made. "Now we'll fasten it to the branch."

The tree trunk was too fat for the boys to shin up, but Freddie had an idea how to attach the rope.

"Dad, I can stand on your shoulders and reach the branch," he suggested.

"Fine," his father said, bending down so Freddie could climb onto his shoulders.

"Please be careful," Mrs. Bobbsey pleaded as Freddie teetered a little.

"Don't worry, Mother," Freddie said. "Dad has hold of my ankles."

Flossie giggled. "This is like a circus act," she said as Nan tossed the vine rope to Freddie.

The little boy was now directly beneath the limb, with the rope clutched in his hands. He reached up and tied the ends to the strong branch.

"Please be careful," Mrs. Bobbsey pleaded

"There. That does it!" Freddie exclaimed when he finished the job. Flexing his knees, he reached down to grasp his father's hands. Mr. Bobbsey somersaulted the boy off his shoulders and onto the ground.

Flossie was the first to run to the swing. It was just the right height from the ground for her to flop onto the rope seat.

"Push me, please," she begged.

Bert gave her a hard shove, and Flossie sailed back and forth. "Whee, this is fun!" she shouted.

After Flossie had had a long ride, Freddie took a turn. "Make believe I'm a plane," he called, gliding back and forth. He made a *whooshing* sound with his lips.

After Freddie decided he had taken a round trip from New York to London, he gave up the swing to Nan. And when all the children had had a ride, Nan said, "Come on, Mother and Dad. Your turns, now."

Mrs. Bobbsey laughed gaily as she took her place on the vine swing. What fun the children had pushing her!

"Oh, oh, not too high!" she squealed after Bert had given her an extra hard shove. "You try it now, Dick."

When Mrs. Bobbsey slowed down and got off the swing her husband took a turn. But he did not swing too high for fear of breaking the vine.

"I think I felt it give a little," Mr. Bobbsey said, getting off. "I may have weakened it, so don't swing too high, children."

Freddie begged the next ride, and started to swing into the air. "See. It's all right, Dad!" he called.

But on the next swing there was a sudden ripping noise. The rope vine parted, sending Freddie tumbling to the ground.

"Oh!" everyone gasped as the boy hit the grass with a thud and rolled over and over.

"Freddie, are you hurt?" Mrs. Bobbsey cried, rushing over to her son, who was sprawled on the ground.

"I guess I'm all right," he said, picking himself up slowly. "Gee, I really bailed out of my plane. Lucky I wasn't over the Atlantic Ocean."

Freddie's good humor made everybody breathe a sigh of relief. His only injury was a skinned elbow. Mrs. Bobbsey bathed it in cool water from a brook near by and applied a small bandage from their first aid kit.

"Now my pilot is as good as new," she said, laughing. "But I think you should rest here awhile before we hike any farther."

As Freddie agreed to play quietly with his twin, Bert said, "Mother, may Nan and I explore the top of that hill over there?" He pointed to a steep wooded section which overlooked the lake.

"All right, but be back in half an hour," Mrs. Bobbsey said.

Bert and Nan started off, climbing over big boulders and threading their way between the scrubby trees which clung to the side of the hill.

"I hope we don't meet that bear," Nan said, glancing from rock to rock. "Oh, what's that?"

Her exclamation startled Bert, but he answered, "It wasn't a bear. Only a rabbit."

"I guess the bear scare has made me jittery." Nan laughed as she tossed her hair from in front of her eyes.

"We're more than halfway up the hill," Bert said, turning to look back at the scene below them.

Mr. and Mrs. Bobbsey and the younger twins were not in sight, being hidden by the heavy growth of trees. But the lake spread out like a lovely diamond nestled in an emerald setting.

"As Flossie would say, it's bee-yoo-ti-ful," Nan said.

"Certainly is," Bert agreed. "It'll look even nicer when we reach the top of the hill."

A few minutes later he and Nan reached the summit. The lake below them seemed even lovelier, partly because there was more of it to be seen.

"But look over there," Nan said, worried, pointing to a bank of dark, low-lying clouds which hung over the southern end of the lake.

"They're storm clouds," Bert replied.

"It seems funny to think of a storm when the sun is still shining," said Nan.

"That's because the wind is from the south," Bert explained. "It won't be long before those clouds will blot out the sun."

"We'd better hurry back and tell Mother and Dad," his twin urged.

"Okay. Let's go. We'll sure get soaked if it starts to pour."

Bert and Nan scrambled back down the hillside. By the time they reached the others, a cool sharp wind had begun to blow. When the older twins told of the storm clouds, Mr. Bobbsey said:

"Come, all of you. We'd better hurry home before the storm breaks!"

"We'll never make it," Mrs. Bobbsey declared.

CHAPTER IX

RAINING CATS AND DOGS

"HURRAY, a storm is coming!" cried Freddie, not the least bit worried about getting wet. A strong gust of wind suddenly bent the tops of the trees with a swishing sound.

When the twins were home in Lakeport, they loved to watch a storm from their front porch. But Freddie thought it was even more thrilling to be caught in one in the woods.

"We'd better get back to our cottage as soon as possible," Mrs. Bobbsey said, gathering up the picnic baskets. "Otherwise we'll all be drenched."

"It may be only a windstorm," Nan said hopefully. "Oh, this is fun." She flung out her arms and the breeze blew through her hair.

Suddenly a strong puff whipped open one of the baskets, picked up the plastic cloth and carried it off like a whirling leaf.

"I'll get it, Mother," Freddie cried, and raced after the plastic cloth.

But it was not easy to catch. Every time the

boy bent over to pick it up, another gust would send it swirling again.

"I'm going to make believe I'm a football player and tackle it," Freddie called out. "Watch me, everybody."

As the others looked on, the excited boy flung himself at the elusive cloth. But before he could pounce on it, the wind blew the plastic cloth out of his reach again.

"Hurry before it scores a touchdown!" Bert said, laughing.

Just then the cloth whirled around like a dancer, covering Freddie's head.

"Ha, now I'm an Indian," the boy shouted, dancing about in the red and blue covering.

In spite of the fun the children were having, Mr. and Mrs. Bobbsey urged them to hurry. The sky grew darker and the wind became a steady roar.

"Come, children, hurry," their mother called as they started back through the woods.

Nan began to worry about something else. She said to Bert, "Maybe by the time we get home, there won't be any camp."

"What do you mean?" Bert asked.

"The bungalow is old and shaky," his twin replied. "It wouldn't take much of a blow to send it into the lake."

"Do you suppose our logs will blow into the lake?" Freddie asked, running beside his father.

"I doubt it. But if they should, it would save all the work of rolling them into the water," his father said with a wink.

"Gracious, how it's blowing!" Mrs. Bobbsey exclaimed.

As the Bobbseys struggled along against the gale, they caught glimpses of the lake. The water was being whipped into white-capped waves which pounded on the shoreline with a loud slapping sound.

"I'm glad we're not out on the lake," Mrs. Bobbsey said.

"It would be great to have a sailboat out there," Bert shouted above the wind.

"You wouldn't have it long," Nan reminded him. "This gale would tear the sails to pieces."

"Look!" Flossie exclaimed. "The leaves are blowing off the trees. There won't be any left!"

It did seem as if the wind would strip all the green from the forest trees as they leaned far over in the terrific blast. But it was the old, dry leaves that were blowing around. The air was filled, too, with flying bits of twigs, some of which pelted down on the Bobbseys.

"Thank goodness there's no thunder and lightning," Mrs. Bobbsey said. But even as she spoke, a low rumbling sounded in the distance.

"Is that the sky giants bowling?" Flossie asked. Once Dinah had told her a fairy tale in which thunder was caused by cloud giants playing tenpins.

No one answered her. Instead, Mr. Bobbsey urged his children to greater speed. "On the double," he commanded. No telling when lightning might strike a tree under which they were passing.

Just then a flash lighted the sky and Freddie began to count. "One second, two seconds, three seconds, four seconds!"

Boom boom came the distant thunder!

"It's four miles away," Nan said. "We still have time to get home before it catches up to us."

The lightning laced the sky and the thunder became louder. Here and there, limbs broken from the trees fell down on either side of the trail. Mrs. Bobbsey looked at her husband as if to ask whether or not it was wise to keep going through the storm. He nodded his head "yes" and they hurried on.

"We must get back to the cottage if we can," he said. But when he came to a little glen, where a split rock formation and old fallen trees formed a sort of cave, he changed his mind. "I think we'd better stay here for a while," he concluded. Large drops of rain had started to pelt down. "It's going to rain cats and dogs in a few minutes and we'll be soaked if we stay out in it."

"Dad," Freddie said, "can we make a shelter with this plastic cloth?"

"That's a good idea," his father replied.

"We must get to the cottage if we can," Mr. Bobbsey said

"It's waterproof and will keep us all dry inside the cave."

Quickly Freddie and Bert gathered some leafy branches that had fallen to the ground and placed them above the old tree trunks that acted as ceiling beams over the cave. Then they spread the cover on top of everything, holding the sides down with large stones.

"Our den is ready!" Freddie shouted as the rain started to come down hard.

The Bobbseys scurried inside their make-shift shelter. It was almost as dry as their own living room at home.

"This is nice," Flossie said, listening to the rain fall on the plastic "roof." "I'd like to live here all the time."

"Like a bear?" Freddie asked. "Oh, that would be fun. Let's pretend we're bears, Flossie."

"Maybe there's a bear in this den already," Flossie said, her eyes growing wide as she peered farther back into the shelter.

The remark made Nan shiver and Bert looked worried. Maybe this was the home of the mad bear!

"I'll go look," Bert said bravely.

He borrowed a packet of matches from his father and went to look. Nan held her breath, but he was back in a minute.

"Nothing here," he reported. "The cave is very shallow."

Outside, the storm continued its fury. The daylight was almost gone. Mrs. Bobbsey glanced at her wrist watch. "We couldn't get home before dark, even if we started now."

"We'll be drenched to the skin if we go now," Bert put in. "I think we should stay."

Mrs. Bobbsey thought for a moment. "It's a hard decision to make," she said, glancing at her husband, who was seated on the ground, his back propped against the rock wall.

"We could stay overnight, couldn't we?" Freddie asked enthusiastically. "I never slept in a cave all night."

"And be eaten by bears? Oh, no!" Flossie exclaimed.

"We could start a fire to keep the bears away," Freddie replied quickly. "I saw it in the movies once."

Mr. Bobbsey chuckled. "Bears or no bears, I'd be happy to stay here," he said. "The pitter-patter of rain will put me to sleep in no time!"

"Oh, Dick," Mrs. Bobbsey exclaimed. "We might catch cold. We have no blankets."

"The rain is coming down in sheets," he said, winking at the children. "Perhaps we could use them."

"Oh, Daddy!" Nan exclaimed. "What an old tease you are!"

"Look!" Flossie cried, pointing outside. "It just rained a puppy dog."

"Impossible," Bert said.

Flossie wagged her head wisely. "Daddy said it was going to rain cats and dogs," she protested. "And I saw one, right over there."

Everybody looked toward the spot where the little girl pointed.

"There *is* something under that tree," Mrs. Bobbsey said. "And it does look like a puppy."

But before she or anybody else had a chance to go out into the downpour, a little animal, grayish brown and with a bushy tail, scurried into a hole under a log.

"It's a groundhog!" Mr. Bobbsey said.

"But you didn't say it was going to rain groundhogs, Daddy," Flossie pouted. "Only cats and dogs."

"Well, this is an unusual storm," her father said, reaching over to grab his small daughter and pull her to his lap. Then he told her that the expression "raining cats and dogs" was just a funny saying which meant it was raining very hard.

"I'm glad," Flossie said, " 'cause I wouldn't want the pussies to hurt themselves by falling out of the sky."

As they talked, the thunder and lightning grew more intense. The younger twins held their hands over their ears to keep out the sound of the crashes. Even Bert and Nan jumped nervously at the loud thunder claps.

"The storm must be passing right overhead," Mr. Bobbsey said.

"Oh dear, I hope it clears up soon," his wife said anxiously.

Suddenly there was a blinding flash and a crackling sound. At the same instant a thunderous blast stunned the Bobbseys!

CHAPTER X

FALLING TREES

AFTER the tremendous clap of thunder which had stunned the Bobbseys, everyone was silent for a few moments. Then Flossie and Freddie screamed.

"Are you hurt?" Mrs. Bobbsey cried quickly.

"N-no," Freddie answered with a sob in his voice. "But, I don't like this! I want to get out of here."

"Me, too!" Flossie's voice quavered. "I want to go home!"

As Mrs. Bobbsey put her arms around the small twins, Bert had the idea of making them laugh to forget their fears.

"Hey," he said, "you two aren't going to cry, are you? It's wet enough outside. Let's keep it dry in here!"

At this, Freddie and Flossie giggled and soon their fears were forgotten, especially when Mrs. Bobbsey suggested that they eat the remainder of the picnic lunch.

There was a large flat rock in the center of their "cave." While Nan set the sandwiches and fruit on this makeshift table, Bert rolled other stones around it to serve as chairs.

Soon everyone was nibbling their second picnic of the day. Flossie declared it was very cozy to sit in the shelter and listen to the storm raging outside. The sharp lightning and booming of the thunder had lessened now.

As it grew darker, everyone found it difficult to see what he was eating. Many mix-ups occurred and everyone laughed gaily at their plight.

"I know what!" Freddie cried. "Let's build a fire. It'll keep us warm and snug and we can tell ghost stories!"

Mr. Bobbsey chuckled. "There's just one thing wrong with that, Freddie. What will we do with the smoke?"

Bert winked at his father. "Of course we could always cut a hole in the plastic roof to let the smoke out," he said.

"And let all the rain come in!" Freddie cried. Then he grinned sheepishly as he realized Bert was teasing him. "Okay," he said. "No fire for us. But it's so dark in here I can't even see what I'm talking about!"

"Neither can we!" exclaimed Nan, laughing.

Flossie yawned and stretched. "Are we going to stay here all night, Mommy?" she asked.

"It looks as if we'll have to," Mrs. Bobbsey said. "You and Freddie can sleep in the leaves at the back of our den. Won't that be fun?"

"Just like the Babes in the Woods story!" Flossie murmured sleepily.

Mr. Bobbsey lighted a match. The small twins curled up in the dry leaves and in a few seconds were sound asleep.

Bert and Nan decided to sit up with their parents for a while. Still thinking of the mad bear rumor, Bert suggested that they roll a stone or branch in front of the opening to the shelter.

"Why should we?" Mr. Bobbsey asked. "We're far enough back so the rain doesn't reach us, and the opening gives us fresh air."

"Well, I just thought there might be some wild animals around here looking for shelter, too," Bert replied.

"No, Bert, I'm sure the animals have found a place to escape the storm long ago. We're perfectly safe," Mr. Bobbsey assured him.

By this time the thunder and lightning had stopped, but the rain continued. The plastic cloth held up amazingly well and only one leak had been spotted so far. It was close to the front of the den, however, so no one was bothered by the slow dripping.

Nan did her best to stifle a yawn, but she finally admitted she was becoming sleepy. When Mrs. Bobbsey suggested that she curl up in the leaves along with Freddie and Flossie, Nan did not protest. It was very quiet and not too cool under the huge, overhanging rock. Presently Nan was sound asleep in the soft leaves.

Bert, however, felt it his duty to stay awake. He was not completely reassured by his father's words about wild animals—especially bears!

"Dad, suppose I take the first watch and you get some sleep. Then I'll wake you and you can take over," he suggested.

"That's very thoughtful, Bert," Mr. Bobbsey replied. "But it won't be necessary. I don't intend to keep any watch myself. Your mother and I will stay up awhile longer, then we'll probably try to get some sleep, too."

The more Bert thought about this, the more he realized his father was probably right. After all, it was doubtful that any animal as large as a bear could come through the opening in the den—even if it were foolish enough to be wandering about in the storm.

"I guess I am pretty sleepy," Bert admitted. "Just call me if you need me, though, Dad."

His father promised that he would and soon Bert, too, was curled up in the leaves at the back of the den. His parents propped themselves against one side of the cave wall and began to talk.

The rain was still pelting down about an

hour later when Mrs. Bobbsey said softly, "Richard, have you noticed that something seems to be worrying Bert?"

"Well, yes," was the reply. "He acted very concerned about wild animals. That's odd, too, because Bert has never been afraid of any animal he'd be likely to meet around here. Do you think we should ask him about it?"

Mrs. Bobbsey was silent for a moment, then replied, "No. I'm sure Bert will tell us if he thinks there is something we should know. You don't suppose he is still worried about those horrid lumbermen, do you?"

Mr. Bobbsey shrugged. "Possibly. I wonder if they came back today. I didn't expect to be away so long."

The steady drumming of the rain on the plastic roof was very soothing, and Mr. and Mrs. Bobbsey found themselves dozing off. Then without warning they were aroused by a sharp cracking sound followed by a tremendous crash!

"What—what was that?" Mrs. Bobbsey gasped.

Before her husband could reply, another crash shook the den!

"Whew! That was close!" Mr. Bobbsey cried.

"But what is it?"

"Trees!" was the terse reply. "The rain has washed the soil from the roots and this heavy wind is toppling them over. Hurry, Mary, we must get under the rock with the children or we'll be crushed!"

In complete darkness they crawled back among the leaves. They were not a moment too soon. A third tree fell with a roar directly across the entrance to the cave. Then there was silence.

Mr. Bobbsey groped for his matches and finally struck one. Some of the tree limbs had lashed at the plastic cover, shredding the front part. But under the rock there was no damage that he could see. Within a short time the rain stopped and the wind died to a whisper. Finally Mr. and Mrs. Bobbsey too fell sound asleep. There was no more disturbance during the night, and the next thing the Bobbseys knew sunlight was streaming through the opening of the cave.

For a moment none of them could remember where they were. Flossie's eyes opened wide and she sat bolt upright. "Oh! My bedroom's all full of people," she said.

This made the others laugh and Flossie finally remembered what had happened. Thankful to have weathered the storm safely, the Bobbseys walked to the entrance of their cave. The twins were startled to find it partly closed until their parents explained about the falling trees. The children had slept so soundly that they had not heard the crashes.

Quickly Bert and his father pulled off enough branches to make a hole through which they could crawl. Once outside the cave, they looked about them in amazement. Now there was no wind, no rain, and the woods were bathed in warm sunshine! But the ground was littered with broken branches, leaves, and here and there a fallen tree.

"Oh, it's good to be out here again," Mrs. Bobbsey cried, brushing the leaves from her dress. "And now for home—home and breakfast!"

"Don't we have anything left from the picnic to eat?" Freddie asked. "I'm starved."

"Me too," said Flossie.

"Well, not much," Mrs. Bobbsey replied.

A dried sandwich did not make a very good breakfast, but Flossie and Freddie seemed to enjoy theirs. They eagerly ate every crumb.

Bert found a little spring. The water was cool and delicious, and after long drinks, the Bobbseys splashed water on their hands and faces. Refreshed, they started on their homeward trip.

After walking about a mile, Mr. Bobbsey called, "Look! There's the lake. We'll follow the shoreline and soon be home."

He pointed to water gleaming in the sunshine through the trees. The twins skipped on ahead, but in a moment Bert stopped and called back to his father. "This isn't Lake

Melrose, Dad. It's only a little old pond."

Mr. Bobbsey hurried to join his son at the edge of the water. For a moment he was silent as he looked across the water.

"You're right, son," he said finally. "We've come the wrong way."

Flossie looked up at her father. "Are—are we lost, Daddy?"

"I hate to admit it," Mr. Bobbsey replied, "but I'm afraid we are!"

CHAPTER XI

A RUINED BUNGALOW

SEEING a look of alarm on Flossie's face, Mr. Bobbsey said hopefully, "We shan't be lost for long."

Nan wondered. None of them had explored the area around Lake Melrose before. In fact, Mr. Bobbsey had never gone far from Kling's camp where his lumber was stacked up.

But her father was full of confidence. "Once we get to the shore of the lake," he said, "it will be easy enough to follow the beach and return to our bungalow."

He led the way through the woods, as the others trailed single file behind him. After a while the small twins began to lag, and Mrs. Bobbsey said, "I don't believe, Dick, that we are going in the right direction after all."

"I'm afraid you're right," the twins' father admitted. "We should have been back at the cave long before this. The woods are so thick I can't get a good look at the sun to find my direction," he complained. "I should have brought a compass."

"Can't you look at the trees and tell the north side from the moss on them?" Bert suggested.

"That isn't always a safe guide," his father replied. "But don't worry, we'll soon find a trail to take us home. We may be a little late for breakfast, but we'll get there sooner or later."

"Listen!" Nan called out suddenly. "I think I hear someone coming."

They all paused, and plainly heard the crackle of underbrush. Who could it be?

"Maybe—maybe it's a big wild animal," Flossie whispered.

"It's a man," Freddie said knowingly. "I can tell by his walk."

A thought came to Bert. Perhaps he was one of the unpleasant lumbermen who wanted to make trouble for his father.

"Hello there!" Mr. Bobbsey called out.

"Hello," the answer came back. "Who are you and what's the matter?"

"We're lost," Mr. Bobbsey shouted, cupping his hands to his mouth. "We want to get back to Kling's lumber camp, where we have a bungalow."

The other person did not answer immediately. Instead he came tramping through the underbrush as the Bobbseys waited intently. Suddenly a tall boy came into view and the Bobbsey twins shouted with joy.

"Bill Stoddard! It's you!" Bert exclaimed.

"Oh, hi!" Bill said, striding up to them with a smile on his good-natured face. "I never expected to find you here. You say you're lost?"

"Yes," said Bert, then introduced his father. "I didn't know your place was so near here."

"Our house isn't as near as you think," the farm boy replied. "I'm out in the woods

hunting our lost cow. But I guess I'll have to give up and go back." Then he added, "What brings you out at this time of day? You must have had an early breakfast."

"We haven't had any breakfast," Nan said.

"I wish we could find your cow," Freddie said. "Then I could have some milk for my cereal—only I haven't any cereal." He grinned.

This made the others laugh and Bill said, "I'm sorry to hear you're hungry. I had a bite to eat before I started looking for our cow. She got lost in the storm last night."

"We'll help you find her," Nan said kindly.

"Thanks, but not right now," Bill said. "I'm going back for my regular breakfast first. Say, won't you folks come along? Mom will be glad to feed you."

"Oh, how wonderful that sounds!" Mrs. Bobbsey cried. "We were out all night in the storm too."

"Out all night?" Bill said. "The whole family of you?"

The Bobbseys quickly told him the entire story and he said, "That's too bad. Well, your troubles will soon be over. But you two kids must be pretty tired," he added, looking at Flossie and Freddie. "Come on, little girl, I'll give you a piggy-back ride." He reached his arms toward Flossie.

"And I'll carry Freddie," Bert chimed in. "We'll get breakfast quicker if we take them this way."

In a few seconds the children were perched on the boys' backs. Bill led the way, and they all headed for the Stoddard farmhouse.

What fun it was for the small twins! Bill and Bert pranced occasionally like skittish horses while Freddie and Flossie hung on tightly, giggling with delight. Soon Bill came to a path he knew well, and the walking became easy for all of them.

"There's a stream up ahead," the boy said. "It's tricky crossing it on the flat stones, so be careful."

Bill and Bert waited at the edge of the stream while the others crossed.

"Don't you think you'd better put the children down and let them walk across?" Mrs. Bobbsey asked anxiously as Bill poised himself to step on the first stone.

"I think we can make it all right," the farm boy said. He leaped from one stone to another, with Flossie clinging tightly to his neck. She screamed excitedly. "There," he said, reaching the other side and called, "Come on, Bert."

Bert stepped gingerly from stone to stone, with his small brother on his shoulders. "Attaboy, one more stone to go," Bill called.

But Bert failed to see a piece of slippery moss on the last steppingstone. His foot skidded into the water and Freddie sailed off his shoulders.

"Look out!" Mr. Bobbsey cried, leaping forward. He reached the boy in time to catch Freddie in his arms. But Bert got his left leg wet up to his knee.

As he staggered onto the bank, he said, "Whew! That was close. Thanks for saving Freddie, Dad."

Mrs. Bobbsey wanted to stop while Bert dried out his shoe and sock, but the boy insisted they keep on.

"We'll be at Bill's house soon, Mother," he said. "I can dry them there."

When Mrs. Bobbsey agreed, the party continued along the woodsy trail, until at last they came to the top of a grassy hill.

"There's our house," Bill said, pointing to a well-kept farm below.

He lifted Flossie off his shoulders and they all hurried down the hill to the farmhouse. Bert and Nan sniffed the air. A tantalizing aroma of brewing coffee and frying bacon reached them as they approached the kitchen.

"Hello, Bill, is that you?" Mrs. Stoddard called as her son opened the door. "Did you find Bossy?"

"No, but I found some hungry folks," the boy said, leading the Bobbseys inside.

"Well, I'm right glad you brought 'em along," said Mrs. Stoddard.

Soon everybody was seated around the kitchen table, enjoying a delicious breakfast. Mrs. Stoddard listened in amazement as the Bobbseys told the story of their night in the storm, and declared they were lucky the falling trees had not hit them.

"I wasn't afraid—'cause I was asleep," Flossie said, sipping some cocoa, and everybody laughed.

After breakfast Mrs. Stoddard told Bill to get the farm truck out of the barn and take the Bobbseys back to their cottage.

"Thank you so much for your hospitality," Mrs. Bobbsey said. "Before we go I'd like to buy some eggs and vegetables from you, if you have them to sell."

"Yes, indeed."

A basket of supplies was purchased, then the Bobbseys piled into the truck. On the way home, the children kept a sharp lookout for the missing cow, but Bossy did not show herself.

"Maybe she'll wander back," Bill said.

Soon the Bobbseys were on familiar ground again. "This is our place," Bert called out. "I can see your lumber pile, Dad!"

"Yes, but where's our bungalow?" Nan cried suddenly. "It's gone! The bungalow is gone!"

"Gone?" Mrs. Bobbsey exclaimed fearfully. "That's impossible."

As they drove nearer, Mr. Bobbsey gave a whistle of surprise. "It isn't exactly gone," he said, "but it's ruined. The wind last night must have blown it down."

Everyone stared in blank astonishment at what had been the Bobbseys' camp home. Now it was wrecked—a pile of twisted rubble!

CHAPTER XII

THE CAMPERS' SURPRISE

EVERYBODY hopped off the truck and ran over to see the tumble-down bungalow.

"Oh dear!" Flossie moaned. "A thunder giant dropped his bowling ball on our camp!"

Despite the grave situation everyone smiled, and Mr. Bobbsey said, "There's just as much damage as if he had." He walked around the pile of sticks and boards that had once been a cottage. He shook his head.

"It's good there wasn't a fire or all our belongings would have been burned up," said Nan.

"It's fortunate, after all, that we weren't here," her mother spoke up. "We were safer in our rocky den."

"We certainly were," Bert agreed, then said to his father, "I'll see if anything else was damaged."

He and Nan hurried off to the shed which housed the Bobbseys' car. The smaller twins, wanting to help too, ran to the water's edge with Bill Stoddard. All five of them came back at the same time.

"Our car's safe!" Bert exclaimed.

"Good!" his father said. "That old shed must be rugged to have withstood such a wind."

"And our boats are all right too," Flossie piped up.

"But they're half full of water," Freddie complained, "and it'll take half a day to bail them out."

"At least they weren't carried off into the lake," Mrs. Bobbsey said. Then she turned sadly toward the wrecked bungalow. "Now I must see about our things."

"We'll help," Bert and Nan offered at once.

"I'll be glad to lend a hand," Bill volunteered.

"Me, too," said Freddie.

"And me!" Flossie cried.

Unable to lift the heavy boards, they began to gather the shingles from the pile of rubble.

"Be careful where you walk," Mrs. Bobbsey warned.

As everyone worked, moving timbers and looking for clothing and utensils, Mrs. Bobbsey said, "I'm glad we had breakfast with you, Bill, because we never would have eaten any here."

"It's good we brought back some food, too," Nan said.

"Oh, look!" Bert cried out as he lifted a large plank. "Our oil stove wasn't even dented."

"Hurray, we can have lunch!" said Freddie, and a moment later shouted, "I found my fire engine!"

"And here are my dolly's clothes," Flossie cried gleefully. "Oh, they're awful dirty."

In a short time a good-sized pile of the Bobbseys' possessions was neatly stacked beside the wreckage. But Mrs. Bobbsey was frowning. Drawing Mr. Bobbsey aside, she whispered, "Dick, a lot of things are missing, especially from the closet."

"Maybe they're still buried," he suggested.

"I'm certain they're not," she replied. "Come, take a look yourself."

By this time the twins had sensed that something was wrong and crowded around asking questions.

"Mother thinks something is still missing," Mr. Bobbsey said. "Let's all search like real detectives."

Not a stick was left unturned in the hunt that followed, but nothing more could be found. Mr. Bobbsey suddenly looked worried. "Some of my things *are* missing," he admitted. "Papers and books that I need in my work."

"And some of your clothes," Mrs. Bobbsey pointed out. "They couldn't have blown away because they were in the closet."

"You mean we had robbers?" Freddie asked excitedly.

"I'm afraid so," his father replied. "Some people certainly have come here and helped themselves."

"Grimes and Lanyard?" Bert asked.

"Perhaps," Mr. Bobbsey answered. "But I had hoped they were more honorable."

"It could have been a tramp," Mrs. Bobbsey said, but Bill assured her there had not been any hoboes around this part of the country in a long time.

"Oh dear, this *is* bad luck," Flossie spoke up quaintly, and gave her daddy a sympathetic hug.

"There's only one thing to do, I guess," said Mrs. Bobbsey.

"What's that, Mother?" Nan asked.

"Get into our car and go home."

"Oh, no!" cried the twins. "Let's stay!"

"But we have no place to eat or sleep."

"We can go back to our nice cave," Freddie said helpfully.

This made the others smile. Nan reminded him that those quarters has been very cramped. "I think Mother's right," she had to agree sadly.

At this Freddie and Flossie looked very downcast. "We're having such good fun here," Freddie said, on the verge of tears.

"I want to stay. I want to stay!" Flossie wailed.

Mrs. Bobbsey sighed and glanced at her husband, who seemed extra calm despite the predicament. Looking directly at the small twins, he said, "Would you like to live in the trees like a pack of monkeys?"

This made Freddie and Flossie laugh. Then he added, "I suppose we might pitch a tent. It wouldn't be the first time."

"A tent!" cried Mrs. Bobbsey. "It would take several days to find a tent the size we need and set it up."

A funny little smile curled Mr. Bobbsey's lips as if he had a great secret he was bursting to tell.

"If I find one, would you mind living in it?" he said. "I think it can be arranged. For my part, I'd like to stay here and see that the logs are properly handled."

"Hurray!" Freddie shouted, and tried to do a cartwheel. But he was so excited he fell over and landed on his back.

"I'd like to stay here," Mrs. Bobbsey replied. "The children like it too, as you can see, but how—"

"Now don't you worry," Mr. Bobbsey said, holding up his hand like a traffic cop. "A tent is here, or so near that it won't take long to get it."

Mr. Bobbsey told his astonished family that he had rented a tent, cots and all necessary supplies in Lakeport, before they had started out, in case the bungalow proved too ramshackle to live in.

"I had them shipped by railroad to a town not far from here. I presume they're still at the station."

"Oh, that's wonderful!" cried Nan.

"You think of everything, Dick," Mrs. Bobbsey said, smiling at her husband. "Of course, we'll stay here now."

Mr. Bobbsey asked Bill if he would drive him and Bert to the station to make arrangements to have the things hauled out.

"Glad to help you," Bill said.

In twenty minutes Bert and his father were

at the railroad station. Mr. Bobbsey went straight to the freight office and gave his name.

"I've come for my camping equipment," he told the clerk.

"Bobbsey, Bobbsey," the man said, pursing his lips and scratching his left ear. "Name's familiar. We had some stuff here for a Mr. Bobbsey but seems to me it's not here now."

Bert groaned when they heard this, and Mr. Bobbsey asked, "It's not here now? What happened to it?"

The clerk said that because nobody had come to claim it, he had marked the camp stuff for return to the store from which it had come.

"I think it was picked up this morning," the man said, pushing his cap back on his head. "But I'll take a look to make sure."

Concerned, the three followed him to the freight platform along the tracks.

"Well, by jimminy," the clerk said, I guess it's still here after all. Is this your order?"

Mr. Bobbsey ran up to examine the crates. "Yes, these are mine!" he exclaimed in relief. "I'll have them picked up."

Since Bill's farm truck was much too small for such a load, Mr. Bobbsey engaged a truck and three workmen to haul the camping supplies out to the lake. He and Bert thanked Bill for his help and said good-by. They would ride out in the big truck.

By the time evening came, what a difference

there was at the Bobbseys' camp! The rubble
had been cleared away and a huge tent
mounted over the old flooring.

Inside, the tent was divided off by curtains of canvas to form little rooms. Flossie
and Freddie excitedly put their toys in place,
and Nan cooked supper.

Later, Bert built a fire outside the tent, and
the family sat around on blankets telling stories
before bedtime. While Nan was making her
story sound very spooky, the stillness of the
forest was broken by a scream.

"Wha-what was that?" Flossie cried out
fearfully.

As the scream was repeated, Mrs. Bobbsey
gasped, "It sounds like a child!"

CHAPTER XIII

A FRIGHTENING CLUE

THE terrifying scream that sounded like a child in danger had frightened the Bobbsey twins so much that for a few moments they could not move.

"Somebody's hurting a poor child," Flossie said. "Stop him, Daddy!"

"Maybe some kid is caught in a wild animal trap," Bert suggested.

"Listen!" whispered Mr. Bobbsey.

For a few seconds there was silence, then the cry was repeated. This time there was no doubt from where it had come, and everyone glanced up toward the branches of a near-by tree.

"Oh, what is it?" Mrs. Bobbsey exclaimed.

Suddenly something rustled and moved among the branches.

"Get out of there!" Mr. Bobbsey cried out. "Scat!" He leaned near the fire to grasp a piece of wood. Then he threw it up among the branches.

Again the strange cry came, this time mingled with a hissing sound. Then the odd, dim shape of an animal slithered down the tree trunk and disappeared into the darkness.

"Whew!" Mr. Bobbsey said, and Mrs. Bobbsey murmured, "Thank goodness."

"Why did you say *scat?*" Freddie asked, wide-eyed. "Was it a cat?"

"Yes, it was a cat. A sort of cat," his father answered. "But not the kind of pussy we have at home. This was a bobcat, or lynx. I didn't realize there were any left in this part of the country."

"Are they dangerous?" Nan asked.

Her father explained that a bobcat is not dangerous if left alone. "They prey on other animals," he said, "but don't attack human beings unless they're cornered."

Freddie was whispering to Flossie, "A bobcat. A Bobbsey cat." Aloud he said, "I suppose the Bobbsey cat saw our fire and wanted to find out who was here."

Everybody laughed, then Bert corrected his brother. "Bobcats aren't related to us Bobbseys," he said.

His mother smiled and said teasingly, "I'm not so sure of that. Once I heard Freddie and Flossie arguing and it sounded something like our friend the bobcat."

The small twins grinned and Flossie asked,

"Is the cat's real name Robert? And is a girl cat called Roberta?"

The children's humor made everyone forget about the fright they had received. Mr. Bobbsey replied, "A bobcat gets his name from his bobbed tail."

"Well, I never want to hear one again, bobtail or not," Nan declared. "It nearly scared me out of my wits."

After the Bobbsey twins had a bedtime snack of crackers and milk, they settled down on their cots. Then, as the fire outside the tent burned lower and lower, they listened to the night noises and the lapping of the lake water.

"Now we really are camping out!" thought Bert, the last one asleep.

He was the first to awaken the next morning. After putting on his jeans and sweater, he hurried to the lake for a bucket of water so all could freshen up. He suggested that they cook and eat outdoors and his father started a fire. Soon bacon was sizzling in the skillet.

"Mrs. Stoddard's eggs sure are good!" Nan exclaimed as the family ate their breakfast.

After the children had burned the paper dishes and made up the cots, Bert took Nan aside and said, "Let's do some detective work today."

"What do you mean?"

"I'd like to get on the trail of the man or men who stole Dad's things," her twin replied.

"Maybe we can find evidence in the woods," Nan said enthusiastically. "If it was those lumbermen, Dad should know about it."

"Right."

The twins spoke to Mrs. Bobbsey. She, in turn, called to the twins' father, who was bailing out one of the boats. He came to the tent and she explained what the children had proposed.

"That's a good idea," their father said. "But I don't want you running into any danger. This is really a policeman's job."

"But it'll be fun playing cops and robbers, Dad," Bert begged.

"Promise to stay near the trail and not go too far into the woods," Mr. Bobbsey said.

"We will," Nan agreed.

"Very well, but be back in an hour," their mother said.

Bert and Nan were elated at the chance to play detective. While Freddie and Flossie were busy floating bits of wood in the lake, the older twins set off along the road behind their tent.

They looked carefully for clues first on one side of the dirt road, then the other. After they had gone a little way, Nan leaned down to pick up a piece of paper. But it proved to be only the label from a tomato can and apparently had been lying there for a long time.

"I don't suppose," Bert said, as the sun beat

down upon them, "that the thieves would have used this road anyhow. They'd go off through the dense woods to avoid being seen."

But Nan did not agree. "The men had plenty of time to get away," she said, "so they probably took the quickest and easiest way. I think we should look farther, Bert."

The two children continued to comb the sides of the old road for another ten minutes. Suddenly Bert cried out, "I've found something!"

Nan raced to his side to look at the white sheet of paper he was holding. Its edges were curled by the morning dew, but the whiteness proved it had not been there long.

"And look at this," Bert said, turning the sheet over in his hands.

"Dad's name!" Nan exclaimed. "It's a piece of his office stationery!"

"Sure enough!" Bert said. "Dad did say some of his papers were missing. I wonder if the thief intends to use Dad's letterhead and forge his name."

"We'd better get back and tell him right away," Nan said.

But Bert was so intent upon the search that he did not want to return at that moment. "We may find another important clue," he urged his sister. "Let's go on a little farther."

Bert folded the paper and put it into his pants pocket. The twins pressed on along the road. But after going another half mile and finding nothing, they stopped.

"I guess we'd better go back," Bert said, shielding his eyes and looking up at the sun. "We've been gone nearly an hour already."

As they turned back, Nan's eyes lighted upon a strange object half hidden in some tall weeds under a tree. Hurrying to pick it up, she cried out, "Bert! A collar with a chain attached to it."

"Jeepers, you're right!" her brother said, turning the collar over in his hands. "If this belongs to a dog, he's a mighty big one."

"It's broken so it must have been torn from the animal's neck," Nan deduced.

Suddenly a thought of Bert's made the hair stand up on the back of his neck. "Nan," he said, breathing hard, "this might have come off the mad circus bear!"

"Oh, goodness," his twin replied, as she glanced toward the edge of the woods. "If the bear is loose around here, we're all in danger at our camp."

Bert held the collar closer to his eyes. "There's printing of some kind on this," he said, "but it's so worn that I can't make it out."

"Here, let me see," his sister said, taking the collar. She studied it carefully and gasped.

"What's the matter?" Bert asked.

"It says 'Empire Circus,'" Nan said, paling. "Oh, hurry, let's get out of this place!"

"It says, 'Empire Circus,'" Nan said

Both children made their way back to the camp as fast as they could go. But on the way, both agreed not to mention the possibility of the bear's being loose.

Their parents were surprised at the articles the children had found along the road.

"That certainly is my letterhead," Mr. Bobbsey said. "But I don't quite understand about the animal collar and chain."

"Bill Stoddard told me a circus bear got away but was caught," Bert spoke up.

"Then I guess this belonged to the bear," Mr. Bobbsey commented, and nothing more was said.

Flossie and Freddie meanwhile had tired of sailing their "boat" twigs and now were playing house. Flossie had put her rag doll, Baby Shiny Eyes, to sleep under a tree. Freddie was holding a small fishing rod off the dock.

"I'll catch some little minnows for lunch for us and Shiny Eyes," he told his sister as she joined him.

Flossie watched him for some time, then pretended she heard her baby cry. "I'll go get her," the little girl said. A moment later she came racing down the slope.

"She's gone, she's gone!"

"Who?" asked Nan, coming out of the tent.

"My doll!" Flossie cried. "Shiny Eyes is gone! Somebody took my doll!"

CHAPTER XIV

THE WOODEN DOLL

TEARS streamed down Flossie's cheeks as she kept repeating, "Shiny Eyes is gone. I've looked and looked, but she's gone!"

"Please stop crying, Flossie," Nan said, drying the little girl's tears, "and tell me exactly what happened."

Flossie managed to stammer out her story about putting her doll under a tree and how, when she went to get her, Shiny Eyes had disappeared.

"Maybe Freddie hid it just to tease you," Nan suggested, but Flossie shook her golden curls, saying that Freddie had not left the waterfront.

The conversation was overheard by Bert, who sat on a log some distance away, whittling a reed. He was trying to make one on which he could play a tune.

Nan and Flossie walked over to him and asked if he had seen anyone take the doll. Bert shook his head, but he gave Nan a knowing look. When his little sister glanced away, he made motions with his lips as if to say:

"Bear!"

His twin nodded and both looked off worriedly into the woods.

At this moment Flossie began to cry. "Shiny Eyes was my favorite camp doll!" she wailed. "I'll never, never see her again!"

Helplessly, Bert and Nan looked at each other. How could they comfort Flossie?

Suddenly Bert's eyes sparkled. "Tell you what, Floss, I'll make another doll for you."

The little girl choked off a sob and looked wide-eyed at her brother. "M—make one? There's nothing to make one with 'round here."

Bert smiled. "Don't be too sure, Sis," he said mysteriously. "You'll have a brand-new doll by lunchtime. I promise."

Flossie looked very doubtful, but when Bert took out his pocket knife and began hunting for a thick branch, she too smiled.

"Ooh!" the little girl squealed. "You're going to whittle me a dolly, aren't you?"

"That's right."

Bert selected a branch about three inches thick and about ten inches long. First he scraped off the bark, then sat down with his back against a big tree and began whittling. Soon Freddie joined the group. He leaned over very close to watch the operation.

"Careful, Freddie," Bert warned as the little boy bent too close to the flashing knife. "I'll be whittling your nose in a minute."

Freddie jumped back grinning and the children settled down beside Bert to watch him work. Slowly the doll began to take shape: a round head, square shoulders, and the first suggestion of arms.

Nan broke the absorbed silence when she asked, "Bert, how long will the doll be from her shoulders to her feet?"

"Oh, about eight inches, I'd say," was the reply.

"And two inches or so around the body?"

"Yes, about that. Why?"

"Because I'm going to go cut out a dress for her while you're working here," Nan replied.

"Then I can fit it and sew the seams after she's all carved."

Nan jumped up and ran to the tent. In a few minutes she returned with a bright red and white plaid dish towel, a piece of chalk, a pair of scissors, and a tape measure.

"This towel is frayed, so Mother said we could have it."

Nan placed the gay material on the grass and began measuring very carefully, then marking with the chalk.

Flossie's eyes darted from her brother's knife to Nan's scissors as her sister began snipping out the pattern she had fashioned. Half an hour later, Bert put down his knife and held the doll off, looking at his handiwork critically.

Flossie was impressed. "Why—she looks almost alive!" she whispered. Bert grinned modestly, and Nan and Freddie agreed that it was a lovely doll.

"Let's take it back to the tent to finish," Nan suggested.

By this time Flossie was so excited at the prospect of a brand-new doll that she danced all the way back to the tent!

Mrs. Bobbsey was called in to admire the little figurine. She exclaimed over it in delight, then offered to draw a face on the doll. Flossie found crayons in her suitcase and her mother started. She put on a smiling mouth, a tiny nose, and big blue eyes. When dark eyebrows and lashes had been penciled on, Flossie's doll seemed about to laugh out loud.

Meanwhile Nan finished the fine stitching on the little dress and finally it was slipped over the doll's head. It fitted perfectly!

"Boy, we ought to go in the doll-making business!" Bert exclaimed, amazed at the family's handiwork.

Only Freddie seemed dissatisfied. "She's nice," he said slowly, "but isn't she sort of bald?"

Giggling, everyone had to agree that the doll did need something on her head. "I might crayon some hair," Mrs. Bobbsey offered.

Freddie agreed that this might help, but he had another idea. "Follow me, everybody," he said mysteriously.

He dashed to the boat dock with Nan, Bert, and Flossie right behind him. Kneeling at the end of the pier, Freddie pointed to some small lily pads growing in the water a few feet away.

"I think one of these would make a pretty hat for the doll," he said. "Bert, hold the back of my shirt while I reach out for one."

Laughing, Bert took a firm hold of his brother's shirt and Freddie leaned way, way out beyond the dock. Just as his fingers closed on the nearest lily pad, there was a loud *ger-lugg!*

Freddie tried to pull back, but too late! A large bullfrog leaped straight up in the air and smacked into Freddie's nose!

"Wow!" cried the little boy and only Bert's firm grip on his shirt saved Freddie from toppling into the water.

Weak with laughter, Bert, Nan and Flossie managed to tug their brother back onto the dock. Still gasping, Freddie exclaimed, "Where did he come from? That old frog must have been sitting on the lily pad all the time and I didn't even see him!"

Much to everyone's surprise, Freddie had held onto the lily pad, and now he began folding it carefully to form a little peaked hat. He gave it to his twin, who carried the hat back to the tent and proudly placed it on top of the doll's head.

"A pixie hat!" exclaimed Flossie. "Freddie, it's bee-yoo-ti-ful!"

"She looks sort of like Robin Hood to me," Bert said.

"What will you name her, Flossie?" her mother asked.

The little girl puzzled over this for a few moments. "Well," she said, "my dolly looks like a pixie to me, and like a robin to Bert, so I'm going to call her Pixie Robin! And she's the nicest camp doll I ever had!"

Mr. Bobbsey returned at lunchtime. The younger twins were still puzzling over the

strange disappearance of Shiny Eyes. Who—
or what—could have taken her, they asked
their father.

"It's certainly a mystery," he said, "and I
can't even guess what happened unless some
stray dog carried off your dolly. But I'm sure
she'll turn up, Flossie."

Flossie finally ceased to be upset over it.
Pixie Robin had claimed the little girl's heart,
at least for the time being.

Next morning all the Bobbseys hiked to the
Stoddard farm to buy fresh milk, eggs, butter,
and meat. They had a pleasant chat with Mrs.
Stoddard, in which she told them that the missing cow had been found. As they were about
to leave, Bill came from a near-by field, his
arms laden with ears of sweet corn.

"Oh, let's buy some," Nan begged her
mother. "We can have a corn roast."

Mrs. Bobbsey purchased several dozen ears.
That evening, Bert built a fire at the water's
edge and the unhusked ears were put into the
hot ashes. How delicious the corn tasted with
lots of freshly churned butter!

"Never since I was born," Nan chanted,
"have I tasted such good corn."

"I'm full as a balloon," said Freddie, pat-
ting his stomach and getting up to walk
around.

Even after everyone had eaten as much as
he possibly could, enough ears of raw corn re-

mained for lunch the next day. These were placed in a heap near one corner of the tent.

About eleven the following day Nan went for the ears of corn. A few seconds later, Mrs. Bobbsey heard her gasp.

"What's the matter?" her mother asked.

"An animal is eating our corn!" Nan cried. "An animal that's wearing a black mask and gloves!"

CHAPTER XV

FIRE!

"A MASKED, gloved animal!" Mrs. Bobbsey exclaimed. "What can it be?"

"Ho ho!" laughed Bert, who had overheard his twin's exclamation. "A masked bandit, eh? Well, I'll fix him!"

"Quietly now," cautioned Mrs. Bobbsey. "If we scare him off, you won't see him."

On tiptoes, the three walked out of the tent and around a corner. There, sitting on its haunches, was an animal with a long pointed nose. A band of black fur ran across the eyes and under the chin. The rest of its fur was gray, but its tail was ringed with bands of white.

As Nan, Bert, and Mrs. Bobbsey watched, the animal stripped the husk from an ear of corn with its front paws. They did look exactly like small, black-gloved hands!

Bert snickered. "It's a raccoon! Nan, don't you know a raccoon?"

At his words, the little animal dropped the corn and scuttled away in fright.

Nan grinned ruefully. "I suppose I should have known what it was right away," she admitted. "I've seen pictures of raccoons, but finding him stealing our corn, I guess my imagination ran away with me."

Laughing, Mrs. Bobbsey remarked, "That black fur around its eyes and those

black hands do make the raccoon look like a masked bandit!"

"He's sure clever with those hands—er— paws, I mean," Bert said.

"Hands is really the right word, I think," his mother replied. "No other animal's paws are so nearly like our own, except possibly the monkey's. And the raccoon does use them to good advantage. Did you know that he washes his food before he eats it?"

"That's right!" Bert exclaimed. "I remember reading that the raccoon dips all his food in a stream or lake to wash it. In fact, green corn is the only thing he doesn't wash."

"Pretty smart animal!" Nan said. "He knows that the corn is kept clean inside its husk, just like a banana is in its skin, so he doesn't have to wash it."

Mrs. Bobbsey examined the ears of corn carefully. Only a few had been gnawed by the visitor, so there were plenty for lunch. Nan carried them inside the tent.

Bert stood staring in the direction the raccoon had taken. "I'd sure like to see him wash some food," the boy thought.

He decided to track the little animal and see if he could locate its nest. Going softly through the woods, Bert spotted a hollow tree which looked like an ideal home for raccoons. He was about to investigate it, when he happened to notice marks in the mud on the edge of a near-by pond. They looked as if they had been made by a baby's foot.

"I'm on the right track," Bert told himself and moved closer.

He remembered reading that raccoons' hind feet make marks just like these. The little animals walk with their heels on the ground, not up on their toes like horses, cows and dogs.

Creeping around a clump of bushes, Bert saw two raccoons wade into the shallow pond and feel about on the bottom with their hands. As he watched, they both caught and killed frogs, which they carefully washed and ate. Then the raccoons waded to shore and pulled up some roots of plants growing near the edge of the pond. These they swirled about in the water and munched on them happily.

Bert decided to look into the hollow tree. There might be some young raccoons in it, although he knew it was too late in the season to find any babies. Standing on tiptoes, Bert looked into the nest through a hole high up in the trunk. No raccoons were in it.

As Bert stepped back and looked down, something on the ground near his feet caught the boy's eye.

"Well, of all things!" Bert exclaimed. "How did Flossie's doll get here?"

On the way back to the tent, Bert decided that one of the raccoons must have stolen Shiny Eyes from under the tree. But what a strange thing for a raccoon to steal!

When Flossie saw Shiny Eyes in her brother's arms, she squealed with delight and clutched the doll to her. "Shiny Eyes! You've come back!" she cried. "Oh, Bert, where did you find her?"

Bert's story about finding the doll and his conclusion that the raccoons must have stolen her made Freddie and Nan laugh. Mr. Bobbsey, however, told the children that it was quite possible that Bert was right. He explained that trappers use shiny bits of metal instead of food as bait in their raccoon traps.

"You see," their father said, "raccoons are as curious as cats. Anything bright and shiny attracts them. The little pieces of metal glitter in the sunlight and the raccoon just can't help coming closer to investigate. But when he tries to pick up the metal, the trap is sprung."

"Then that old raccoon probably saw the sun shining on Shiny Eyes' shiny eyes!" Freddie exclaimed, and the others laughed.

"Or something like that," Mr. Bobbsey said, with a chuckle. "Well, that mystery is solved, anyway. But we still have one more mystery."

"What's that?" Flossie asked, trying to decide which doll to hug first, Shiny Eyes or Pixie Robin.

"The mystery of why Grimes and Lanyard never returned," was her father's reply. "If they collected their wages, I should think they would have let me know."

"If they took your papers and some of your clothes," said Bert, "maybe they're afraid to come back."

"Maybe," Mr. Bobbsey said doubtfully.

Nan was thinking of still another mystery. Finding the collar and chain from the circus was part of it. Though there had been no sign of the bear, she was still afraid that it might not have been caught.

That afternoon, Mr. Bobbsey and Bert raked the grounds around the tent thoroughly. The twigs, leaves, and branches blown down by the storm had made their camp site look very cluttered and messy. They had waited until now to be sure the debris was thoroughly dry so it could easily burn.

To this pile they added the broken wood from the shattered bungalow and soon an enormous heap of brush and wood was formed on the beach.

"This seems like a good day to burn it," Mr. Bobbsey said to his son.

The wind had died abruptly that morning. Not a ripple of water marred the glassy surface of the lake.

"It should be as safe today as anytime," Bert agreed. "Especially with lake water handy if some sparks should fly."

As an extra precaution, however, father and son dug a wide, shallow trench completely around the brush heap and connected this with a ditch to the water's edge. Finally Mr. Bobbsey struck a match and touched the flame to the brush. Bert did the same on the opposite side.

In the still, dead air, the flames shot straight up toward the sky. What a huge blaze it was! The crackling and snapping of the brush could be heard over the roar of the flames.

Mr. Bobbsey watched it awhile, then said, "I'm sure there's no danger of the fire spreading, and I have some papers to work on in connection with the lumberyard. But Bert, will you stand guard until this is completely out while I'm in the tent?"

"Sure, Dad," Bert agreed readily.

In case a spark should fly, he had filled one of their water buckets with sand and one with lake water. These were close at hand and Bert felt confident he could manage.

As Bert patrolled the area around the fire, he suddenly felt cooler.

"That's funny," he mused.

He turned his face toward the lake. His heart leaped. A breeze had sprung up!

Whirling about, Bert turned to the blazing pile. The flames were already bending in toward the brush at the edge of the woods.

A sudden overpowering gust of wind slapped Bert on the back, forcing him a few steps toward the blazing heap. As he regained his balance, Bert stared about him in terror.

Sparks from the fire whirled up and over the brush, and whole branches whipped off the pile, soaring straight for Mr. Bobbsey's logs!

"Dad!" shrieked Bert. Come quickly!"

CHAPTER XVI

DANGER

BERT'S cries of alarm about the fire quickly brought Mr. and Mrs. Bobbsey and the other twins to the scene of the roaring blaze.

"Oh, this is dreadful!" cried Nan. "How did it happen?"

"The wind," said Bert, dashing off for another pail of water.

Mr. Bobbsey picked up a large stick and tried to beat out the spreading flames. In the meantime, Mrs. Bobbsey grabbed the pail of sand, threw it on the flames, and then went for some water. Flossie ran to the tent for her sand pail.

"Hurry!" Mr. Bobbsey called to his helpers. "We've got to douse this fire before it reaches the pile of lumber!"

Freddie, who had also run to the tent, now returned with his toy fire engine.

"Don't worry, Daddy," he called out importantly, "I'll have this out for you in a minute."

"That's fine, little fat fireman," called his father, who had given this nickname to Freddie some time before. The little boy ran excitedly to the lake to fill up the engine with water.

All this time Mr. and Mrs. Bobbsey and Nan had been running back and forth to the lake to fill their pails and toss the water on the crackling fire. It seemed to make little impression on the flames.

"Oh dear!" Mrs. Bobbsey cried. "It's gaining on us."

"We'll have to work faster!" her husband replied.

"Look," Bert called out, pointing to a tongue of flames licking along the grass toward the tent. "All our things will burn up if we don't put that out!"

Everyone turned to fight this as Freddie hurried up with his fire engine full of water.

Squirt! Squirt! went the engine. There was a hiss of steam.

The flames died down long enough for the children to trample the charred grass with their feet.

"Hurray! We put it out!" Freddie cried as the white smoke curled up around his sandals.

"Good boy!" his father replied. "We've saved the tent, but the blaze is gaining over this way."

He pointed to the flames which shot up as high as a man's head and continued to eat their

way toward the woods and the piles of timber. The air became so hot that it scorched the Bobbseys' faces.

"Stand back!" Mrs. Bobbsey warned, as sparks started to fall all about them. A hot ash fell on Nan's arm and she cried out in pain.

Mrs. Bobbsey examined Nan's arm with concern.

"It will be all right, dear," she said with relief. "I'll put some ointment on it later so it won't blister. You take Freddie and Flossie down to the boat and row them out on the lake."

"We want to stay and help," the small twins chimed in unison.

"You'll all be safer there until the fire is out," Mrs. Bobbsey said firmly. "Hurry!"

Nan obeyed. Grasping the children's hands, she ran to the dock. Mr. and Mrs. Bobbsey and Bert continued to work feverishly as Nan helped her brother and sister in the boat. But it was all she could do to keep the small twins there, as they wanted to go back and fight the fire. Nan gave the boat a swift shove out from the shore and jumped in herself.

Mr. and Mrs. Bobbsey and Bert ran back and forth with full pails and empty pails. But all the water they splashed on did not seem to do much good.

"It's getting away from us, I'm afraid," Mr. Bobbsey said wearily, pausing for a moment's rest.

"Oh, Dick, what shall we do now?" his wife sobbed. "All your lumber will burn and the whole forest may go."

Just then a loud shout came from among the trees, and several men and boys ran forward.

"We'll help!" they cried.

As they drew closer, the Bobbseys saw that they carried brooms and buckets. Racing alongside of an older man whom he closely resembled was Bill Stoddard. "That must be his father," thought Bert.

"We saw the smoke," Mr. Stoddard explained. "Guess you started a fire that got away from you in this tricky lake wind."

Without pausing for a reply, the men and boys went to the lake for water.

"We'll form a bucket brigade," Mr. Stoddard called.

The men formed a straight line which stretched from the lake to the outskirts of the fire. The man nearest the lake filled the pails with water and then passed them to the man next to him. Rapidly the pails changed hands on up the line until they reached Mr. Bobbsey, who stood at the very end. Mr. Bobbsey threw the water on the fire with as much force as he could muster.

"We're getting it under control!" he shouted after a few minutes.

The flames were now only waist high. Breaking their line formation, the men grabbed brooms and beat the fire with all their might.

"We're winning!" Bert cried, as he and Bill, standing side by side, smothered the flames.

"There!" Mr. Stoddard exclaimed, as he threw on a final bucket of water. "I guess it's out and I'm sure glad it was no worse."

"So am I," Mr. Bobbsey replied, as everybody sat down to rest. "We could never have done it without your help. I don't know how we can thank you. I'll never start another fire so near the woods again—I didn't know about that lake breeze. It started up very suddenly. Fortunately Bert was here to warn us."

When Nan saw that the fire was out, she rowed back to the dock. In a few minutes she and the smaller twins joined the others.

Nan wet her handkerchief in the lake and wiped Mrs. Bobbsey's hot face. "You're a real heroine, Mother," she said proudly.

"You bet she is," the others agreed.

"She's a lady fireman," Freddie said. "My mother takes after me," he added, throwing out his chest.

When everyone had rested a few minutes, Mr. Bobbsey rose and shook hands with Mr. Stoddard and the other men who had assisted him.

"I'm a thousand times obliged to you folks for your help. My lumber would have been destroyed and no telling what else," he said gratefully.

"Don't mention it," Mr. Stoddard said, daubing at his sooty face with his handkerchief. "All country folk are good neighbors in times like this."

"And I'm glad of it," Mrs. Bobbsey said with a smile. "Now if you men and boys will wait for a moment, I'll make you all some cool lem‑ onade."

"That sounds mighty good," Mr. Stoddard said. "We sure are thirsty enough for it."

"Goodie, goodie!" Freddie and Flossie shouted. They went with their mother to help prepare the drinks.

While this was being done, Bert and Nan talked with Bill Stoddard about the collar and chain they had found along the road. At the mention of the Empire Circus, Bill said that it had passed that way several weeks before.

"But I don't know where it is now," he said.

"Could you find out?" Nan asked.

"I think so. The man at the railroad station might know where it went, because the animals were sent in freight cars."

"Would you do us another favor, Bill?" Bert asked.

"Sure thing."

"When you get to the station and find out where the circus is, would you telephone the circus manager and ask him if they really did find their lost bear?"

Bill agreed to do this, just as Freddie and Flossie approached the group with a pitcher of lemonade and paper cups. While the "fire‑ fighters" drank, Mr. Bobbsey told them about the theft at their shattered bungalow.

"We thought a tramp might have stolen our things," Mrs. Bobbsey said.

"It wasn't a tramp at all," said a boy called Henry Armstrong.

"They all looked at him in surprise."

"How do you know, Henry?" Mr. Stoddard asked.

"Because it was two lumbermen," the boy replied calmly.

"Lumbermen!" Mrs. Bobbsey exclaimed, looking at her husband. "Tell us about it, Henry."

Henry explained that he had been hiking through the woods with his dog the day before, and had seen two men in a canoe some distance below the Bobbseys' camp.

"I could hear them talking," Henry added. "One said, 'That was a good haul we made from that wrecked bungalow!'"

"Goodness!"

"And that isn't all," Henry continued. "I heard the other one say, 'Yes, and we got a lot more than food.' Then his friend told him to be quiet in case somebody was around."

"They didn't see you?" Mr. Bobbsey asked.

"No."

"Well," Mr. Stoddard said firmly, "we can't have things like that happening around here! I'm a deputy constable. I'm going to see about these men!"

But before he had a chance to move, Bert called out, "Look! Here come some lumbermen now!"

CHAPTER XVII

A MUDDY MIX-UP

"OO-OO, maybe the bad lumbermen are with those men, Daddy!" Flossie cried fearfully.

And Freddie said, "Maybe they've come to take your logs!"

Certainly the group of approaching men looked rough enough in their work clothes. Each one carried some tool of the lumber trade, an ax, a crowbar or a peculiar-looking hook used for turning logs over.

As they drew closer, Mr. Bobbsey said, "Lanyard and Grimes aren't among them." The twins were relieved.

Mr. Stoddard asked Henry if any of these men were the two he had overheard talking in the canoe.

The farm boy shook his head. "I didn't get a very close look at 'em. I really don't know."

"Mr. Stoddard," said Mr. Bobbsey in a low voice, "there may be trouble with these men even if they're not the ones who took my things."

"What sort of trouble?"

Mr. Bobbsey quickly explained that the men might be friends of Grimes and Lanyard, who had threatened to take his logs in payment for wages they claimed he owed them.

"We won't let 'em!" the farmer exclaimed.

By this time the leader of the approaching group, a tall fellow, was within talking distance. He stopped, gazed curiously at the group of firefighters, and said, "I'm looking for a Mr. Bobbsey."

"That's my name," answered the twins' father.

"Glad to meet you. My name's Todd—Sam Todd," the tall man went on. "I received word that you wanted a gang of men to float some logs down to your mill on Lake Metoka."

A sigh of relief came from Mr. Bobbsey and his family. "I'm certainly happy to see you," he told Sam Todd, who was the foreman. Then he said to Mr. Stoddard, "It's all right. These are the men who are going to raft my lumber. They aren't the ones who claimed I owed them money."

Mr. Bobbsey told the foreman how he wanted the logs made into rafts and floated down the lake. Flossie and Freddie mentioned the windstorm, the fire, and the bad lumbermen.

"Well, you've had plenty of excitement at camp," Mr. Todd said. "Those fellows ought to be caught."

"We're going to get right after them," Mr. Stoddard declared, "as soon as I round up some more of my neighbors to help me."

"Well, whether or not you catch those two," Mr. Todd said, "they still won't be able to take Mr. Bobbsey's logs, because we're going to have them in the lake before you know it."

A few minutes later, Mr. Bobbsey left with the farm men and boys in search of Grimes and Lanyard. But before Bill Stoddard set off, Bert asked him to be sure to telephone the circus manager.

"I won't forget," the boy promised.

"Good luck on capturing the thieves!" Bert shouted, wishing he might have gone along.

The thieves were soon forgotten by the twins because of the activity at their camp. The lumbermen, under Sam Todd, first made a camp for themselves a little farther down the lake from where the tent stood. They built a lean-to, a sort of three-sided shack, of tree branches.

As the children looked on, Sam said, "It's so warm at night we don't need much shelter."

"But what are you going to eat?" Freddie asked, not seeing any food.

"Pork and beans, mostly," came the reply. "We do our own cooking," he went on, "but we're not much good at making desserts."

"I'll make one for you if we have any ingredients left," said Nan. "But we lost a lot of food when the bungalow collapsed."

"We'll get along," the foreman said, smiling, as he directed the men to start the rafting job.

Nan and Flossie watched for a few minutes. How skillfully the men rolled the timbers into the lake and nailed them together with long strips of saplings!

Then Nan told herself, "I'm going to see if I can find something to make a dessert for these men, and I'll do it right away!"

Flossie's mind was wandering along the same lines. She would have fun making a pie, only it would be of mud and baked in the sun. She skipped off after Nan. The little girl found a small pan and a spoon in the tent, then went outside to bake a chocolate mud pie.

Meanwhile, Nan had discussed the dessert with her mother. "All I have for the purpose is a muffin mix," Mrs. Bobbsey said.

"I can make a cake with that," said Nan. "And we do have chocolate."

As Nan worked, her younger sister was very busy with her own "baking."

"I'm going to give this to the lumbermen too," she thought, laughing. "They'll think it's real."

By the time Nan had removed the two layers of her cake from the oven, Flossie had her mud pie ready and neatly wrapped. Then she helped Nan prepare the icing for the real cake, licking the spoon and the pan in which it had been made.

"My, that's a wonderful-looking cake," Mrs.

Bobbsey said as she helped Nan put it into an old cookie box. "I'm sure the workmen will like it."

The two girls set off, Flossie carrying the mud pie about which she was very mysterious. Nan supposed it was a package of crackers. Arriving at the lumbermen's camp, they found the men washing up after a hard afternoon's work.

"We have a cake for you," Nan said proudly.

"And a pie," Flossie added.

Flossie skipped forward and presented her package to Mr. Todd.

"It's making my mouth water already," the tall workman said as he opened the box. But suddenly his face fell. "Oh—I—ah—thought —" he stammered as the others pressed around him. "This is a mud pie! I suppose yours is the same," he said to Nan, reaching for the box she held in her hand.

Nan was too amazed at Flossie's trick to say anything. She handed him her box without a word. Mr. Todd opened it and gave a surprised shout.

"Hey, boys, this is no joke! This is a real cake, with chocolate icing! Thank you very much, Nan. Well, little girl," he said, tweaking Flossie's nose, "I'll forgive you now for playing a trick on me."

The workmen's laughter brought Freddie and Bert running up from the lakeside, where they had been playing with some short logs.

"I guess it's time for us to go home," Nan said to them, after they had heard the joke too.

When the Bobbseys reached their own camp they found that their father had just arrived after searching for Lanyard and Grimes in the woods.

Bert and Freddie cheered their father up by telling of the progress made by Mr. Todd and his men with the rafting. After supper Mr. Bobbsey strolled over with them to see for himself. He was very pleased.

Early the next morning the Bobbseys heard a shout down the trail, and saw Bill Stoddard riding up on his bicycle. "I have news about the bear," he said excitedly.

"Did they find him?" Bert asked.

"No. He's still loose," Bill answered. "But that's not the most important news."

"Tell us," Nan said eagerly.

"The circus bear is named Bobo. He's real tame and does funny tricks. And there's a reward for his return!"

When he had left, Freddie said to his brother, "Let's make a raft out of those short logs and pole our way along the shore."

"Why?" Bert asked.

"To look for Bobo. Bears like fish, and maybe Bobo is fishing for his breakfast."

"Good idea!" Bert said. "We'll make a raft right away!"

CHAPTER XVIII

PIRATES

BEFORE starting to build their own raft, Freddie and Bert first watched the lumbermen fasten the big logs together by nailing slender saplings crosswise to several of them.

Then the boys assembled small logs for themselves. Having picked what they needed, Bert asked Sam Todd if he might borrow a hammer and some nails.

"Sure, son," was the reply. "Help yourself."

While Freddie held each sapling across the logs, Bert nailed it fast. At last they had a sizable raft with crossbars at each end and in the middle.

"Let's try it out!" Freddie cried eagerly, and the brothers pushed and hauled their raft to a little cove some distance up the shore from the tent. It floated perfectly and supported both boys easily when they hopped aboard.

Bert fastened an oar from one of the rowboats to one end of the raft. With this as a rudder, the raft could be steered from side to side.

"We'll need boxes to sit on so our feet won't get wet when the waves wash aboard," Bert said thoughtfully. "I know! We can use two of the packing cases that the cots came in."

Soon these were nailed into place on the raft.

At lunch, the whole conversation was about the cruise down the shoreline in search of the missing bear.

"We'll explore just like Robinson Crusoe," Freddie said excitedly. "And we'll have to pack some food in case we're shipwrecked!"

While Freddie put generous quantities of bread, meat, and fruit in a picnic hamper, Mrs. Bobbsey looked on in amusement.

"But why all the food?" she asked. "You'll be back for supper."

Bert grinned. "Oh, sure, Mother. But you know Freddie and food! Don't worry, we'll bring back everything we don't eat."

Nan and Flossie went with their brothers to the little cove where the raft had been moored to a stump. When the picnic hamper was stowed aboard, Freddie cast off the mooring line, and Bert used a stout sapling to pole the raft out into the main body of the lake.

"Bring back the trick bear!" Flossie called from the shore.

"Good luck!" Nan said, waving to the boys as they poled the raft around a tip of land and disappeared from view.

Hugging the shoreline, Bert steered the raft

along with the current while Freddie, one hand shading his eyes, scanned the horizon.

"Hey, Freddie," Bert finally said, "you're supposed to be watching the beach for signs of the bear! What are you looking across the lake for?"

"Shh!" Freddie said. "I'm keeping a sharp lookout for pirate ships! Ho! There's one now!" The little boy pointed excitedly to something in the water some distance away.

"Where?" Bert asked, looking over the water. "I don't see anything."

"It's gone now," Freddie said in disgust. "Those pirates are tricky. Maybe it's a ghost ship and disappears when you look at it!"

Bert grinned and shook his head. "What an imagination!"

By now the wind on the lake was carrying the little raft faster than Bert could pole it, so he pulled the sapling aboard and went back to the rudder.

Suddenly Freddie jumped off the box and cried, "There it is again! The ghost ship!"

Bert looked in the direction Freddie was pointing. "Hey!" he exclaimed. "There *is* something out there!" He moved the rudder so the raft headed away from shore and toward the object they had sighted.

As they came closer, Freddie's shoulders drooped. "Oh, it's just a canoe!" he cried in disappointment. "And not even a pirate in it!"

"That's funny," Bert mused. "What's an empty canoe doing out here in the middle of the lake?" He guided the raft closer to the drifting boat and said, "Freddie, as we come alongside, grab the canoe. I want to investigate this."

Freddie was first to spot the name painted on the side of the canoe. "Look, Bert!" His brother read the name, *Hide-a-way*.

The raft scraped against the side of the canoe and Freddie grabbed one side, holding the light craft tight against their raft. Bert lashed the rudder in place with a piece of the mooring rope and joined Freddie at the side.

"What's that rolled up under the forward seat?" he asked.

Leaning over, Freddie reached under the seat and drew out a plaid jacket. "Why this is Dad's!" he exclaimed.

"It does look like his," Bert admitted and began to search the pockets. From one he drew out a slim pocketknife with the initials, R.B., carved on the handle.

Bert and Freddie stared at each other. This was the knife the children had given their father on his last birthday.

"The thieves used this canoe!" Bert said excitedly.

"But where are they?" Freddie asked.

After a careful search which revealed nothing further in the bottom of the canoe, Bert looked toward the shore. There was not a camp in sight, but he spied a small stream that emptied into the lake.

"This canoe might have drifted down that stream," he said. "Maybe the men are up there somewhere."

"Are we going up there to get those pirates?" Freddie asked.

Bert thought they ought to do some scouting, but not let the men see them. As he dipped the pole in to send the raft toward shore, Bert felt a moment of panic. He could not reach bottom!

"I guess we'll have to abandon ship," he said. "The wind is blowing us and I can't pole back."

"What'll we do?" Freddie questioned.

"We'll transfer to the canoe," Bert replied, trying to keep calm.

He removed the rudder to use it later as an oar, while Freddie lifted the picnic hamper into the canoe. Then the boys broke off a slat of the largest packing case so Freddie could use it for a paddle.

"Careful!" Bert warned, as his brother climbed into the canoe.

Bert followed him, then shoved off from the raft. Soon the brothers were paddling swiftly toward the stream they had seen.

"Good-by, old raft," cried Freddie. "We'll miss you."

When the boys were still about twenty feet

from shore, they heard a harsh grating sound on the bottom of the canoe.

"We've hit something!" Bert yelled.

The next instant the canoe shuddered to a stop. Bert leaned over and groped in the water.

"It's a tree trunk," he said. "Maybe I can push us off."

As his little brother steadied the canoe, Bert used his oar to shove against the trunk, but it was no use.

"We're stuck fast," Bert gasped. "We'll have to wade ashore. It can't be very deep here since that trunk caught us."

"Wow!" Freddie exclaimed. "We're really shipwrecked. Abandon ship," he ordered, "and don't forget the food! Now I'm Robinson Crusoe and you're my good man Friday."

Bert slipped over the side. The water came only to his waist, so Freddie passed him the food hamper. Then the little boy slid into the water himself.

"Tie Dad's jacket around your neck," Bert ordered. "That's valuable evidence, so we've got to take it along."

Freddie complied and put the pocketknife between his teeth so it would not get wet. Together the brothers struck out for shore.

"Boy, with that knife in your mouth you really look like a pirate," Bert said, grinning. Freddie scowled and tried to look ferocious.

They reached the beach without further

trouble and stretched out on the sand to dry their clothes. The picnic hamper provided a hearty and welcome snack.

Half an hour later, the boys started the trek inland along the stream, still carrying Mr. Bobbsey's jacket, the knife, and the hamper.

It grew darker as the woods closed in about them. They tramped steadily on, following the meandering stream until Bert stopped abruptly, holding up his hand as a signal for Freddie to halt.

"There's something flickering through the trees up ahead," Bert whispered. "Let's get closer, but be quiet. I think it's a campfire and it may belong to Grimes and Lanyard."

On tiptoe, the boys moved toward the firelight, until the trees began to thin out. A clearing could be seen ahead, with a campfire in the center. The boys dropped to their hands and knees and crept forward. Soon they were close enough to hear the voices of two men who were seated near the fire. The flickering light danced over their coarse, sunburned features.

"It *is* Lanyard!" Bert whispered. "And Grimes."

The taller man, Grimes, mumbled something, then snarled, "I told you to make that canoe fast! We'd have been miles away from here by now if it hadn't drifted off."

"Aw, stop worrying," Lanyard retorted. "We'll get the men and if Bobbsey doesn't come across with the money he owes us, we'll take that lumber yet!"

"Shut up!" Grimes hissed. "I heard something over there in the trees." He was pointing straight toward Bert and Freddie!

"Let's get out of here," Freddie whispered in a panic, and slowly the boys began inching back from the clearing.

As soon as they reached a thicker part of the woods, the boys scrambled to their feet and raced back down the bank of the stream. They could hear the men coming after them, but the sand muffled the boys' footsteps somewhat, and Grimes and Lanyard were unable to find them. Gradually the noise of their pounding feet grew fainter and at last died away.

Panting with exhaustion, Bert and Freddie flopped on the sand bank. Bert had dropped the picnic hamper during their headlong flight, but Mr. Bobbsey's jacket was still tied around Freddie's neck and the knife was safely stowed in the pocket of his shirt.

"I guess we outran them," Bert gasped with satisfaction, "but for a while there it was close!"

"I'll say!" Freddie replied weakly.

Suddenly something crashed through the underbrush directly behind them!

Freddie and Bert stiffened.

Was it the missing bear? A wild animal? Or had Grimes and Lanyard followed them after all?

CHAPTER XIX

A STRANGE DANCER

BACK at the Bobbsey tent, Nan was busy repairing the bear's broken collar. If they should find the animal, they could slip it over his head and keep the bear until the circus men came for him.

Mrs. Bobbsey was preparing supper while Flossie, in her bathing suit, was pretending to teach her doll, Shiny Eyes, to swim.

"Look how well Pixie Robin swims!" she scolded.

The wooden doll Bert had carved bobbed about on the lapping waves.

"Now you try it." Carefully Flossie placed Shiny Eyes, face down, in the shallow water. Then the little girl stepped back to see if the doll could do the "dead man's float."

A moment later, she rescued the sodden, sinking toy, wrung it out, and was about to start all over again when Nan called to her.

"Flossie, have Bert and Freddie come back yet?"

"No," was the reply. "They're probably ship-wrecked by now. Freddie was going to play Robinson Crusoe, you know."

Nan laughed and went back to her job. Her mother set the picnic table for supper under some trees which were near the water.

Just as she finished, there were shouts of "Hello!" and Mr. Bobbsey, the Stoddards, and several deputies emerged from the woods. They looked rather discouraged.

"Did you find Grimes and Lanyard, Dad?" Nan asked, jumping up to greet her father. Flossie and Mrs. Bobbsey hurried to join them.

"No, not a trace of the men," he replied. "We scoured the woods for miles around and even went some distance along the lake shore, but no luck."

"Say, where are your boys?" Bill Stoddard asked suddenly.

When Mr. Bobbsey learned that Bert and Freddie had not returned, he became worried. But Mrs. Bobbsey assured him the boys would probably be back shortly, since they had promised to return in time for supper.

Flossie stared at an instrument which Bill Stoddard carried under his arm. "Is that a guitar?" she asked.

Bill grinned. "Well, almost," he replied. "It's really a ukulele. I picked it up when we passed our house on the way here. Thought you might like to hear it."

"Can you play your uke—uke—can you play it?" Flossie asked.

"A little," Bill replied.

He plucked the strings, tuned the ukulele, and then struck up a merry tune. Everyone clapped their hands to the engaging rhythm and Flossie danced a few steps. Soon they were all stamping their feet to the infectious gaiety of the music.

"How about a square dance, folks?" Bill called, and with laughter the deputies, Mr. Stoddard, and the Bobbseys formed a circle for the reel.

Louder and faster the music rang through the woods and the dancers whirled about the beach. Suddenly Bill yelled, "Hey, look!" and pointed toward the trees.

Out from the woods lumbered a black bear with a bright red hunting cap perched on his head.

"Well, of all things!" cried Mr. Stoddard. "Here's a new type of hunter!"

"It must be Bobo!" Nan exclaimed. "And look, he's dancing, too."

As everyone watched, fascinated, the bear took three quick hops, then somersaulted closer. Round and round he whirled, stamping first one foot, then the other.

When he stretched up on tiptoes and did what might be called a bear's pirouette, everyone laughed so hard he could scarcely stand.

"It must be Bobo!" Nan exclaimed

And Bill, doubled over with laughter, stopped playing.

A look of disappointment passed over the bear's face as the music stopped. He stood with one leg still up in the air and a paw dangling peculiarly.

Then, before Bill could play again, Bobo raised his head and sniffed the air. With a happy snort he lumbered over toward the picnic table. One huge paw grabbed an open jar of honey and a long pink tongue scooped into the yellow sticky stuff.

"Oh, Bobo!" Nan cried, as she ran to the tent for the circus bear's collar and chain.

Bill played a few chords on the ukulele and instantly Bobo was on his feet, stamping about and waving the half-empty honey jar. Suddenly the huge animal lumbered straight toward Flossie.

With a scream, the little girl fled to her mother. But Bobo seemed even more startled than Flossie had been. Turning with a speed that was amazing for his size, the bear galloped off and was lost among the trees.

"Oh!" Nan cried as she returned with the collar.

She and Bill ran after Bobo but could not catch him as he lost himself in the shadows. They returned to the others.

Flossie looked somewhat ashamed. "I'm sorry I screamed, Nan," she said. "But when Bobo came right at me I got scared—awful scared!"

Nan smiled at her sister. "That's okay, Flossie. I understand. But next time, remember that Bobo is a trick bear. He wouldn't hurt you, I'm sure."

"That's right," Bill spoke up. "Maybe he just wanted to dance with you, Flossie!"

The little girl's eyes grew wide with excitement. "Ooh! Do you really think so? Then we'll just have to catch him so I can have another chance."

Nan suggested that if Bill played some more music perhaps the bear might return. So once again the rollicking, foot-stamping music rang through the woods. But Bobo did not come back.

At last, Bill laid down his ukulele and grinned. "I guess that's the extent of my repertoire."

"What did he say?" Flossie whispered to her sister.

"He doesn't know any more tunes," Nan whispered back.

"But I like them," her small sister said. She turned to her mother and said in a low voice, "Can't we ask him to stay to supper?"

Mrs. Bobbsey nodded and invited Bill and Mr. Stoddard as well. Both accepted.

"Mrs. Stoddard is entertaining a ladies' church group tonight," Bill's father said, "so my son and I feel sort of left out."

The other deputies said they must be going to their own homes for supper. After promising to return in the morning to continue the search for Grimes and Lanyard—and also the bear, the men left.

The Bobbseys and their guests waited a half hour for Bert and Freddie, but the boys did not come.

"What could be keeping them away?" Mrs. Bobbsey said. "It's beginning to grow dark!"

"Perhaps we should go ahead and eat," Nan suggested, thinking of their guests, and Mrs. Bobbsey agreed.

Even though Nan and Mrs. Bobbsey had prepared a delicious meal, none of the Bobbseys ate very much. They were becoming alarmed. The Stoddards talked about interesting, happy things, hoping to make the others forget their fears for Freddie and Bert.

Flossie had said very little during the course of the meal. The little girl seemed lost in thought until she looked up at her father suddenly and cried, "Daddy! That was your hat Bobo was wearing!"

Startled, Mr. Bobbsey thought for a moment. "I believe you're right! That could have been my hunting cap. I remember now that it was missing from the bungalow after the storm. Good for you, Flossie!"

He hugged his little daughter. "This may be a real clue."

"You mean maybe the bear stole all the things from the bungalow?" Nan asked in astonishment.

"No, Nan," her father replied. "What must have happened was that Grimes and Lanyard dropped the cap somewhere in the woods and Bobo picked it up."

"Or Bobo may even have found their hideout!" Nan cried excitedly.

"It's possible," Mr. Bobbsey replied, rubbing his chin thoughtfully.

"Maybe we could follow the bear's tracks tomorrow and find the lumbermen," Bill suggested with excitement. "Bobo might return to their hideout if he wants more clothes to dress up in."

"That's an idea," Mr. Bobbsey said, "but right now I'm more interested in finding Bert and Freddie than I am in the lumbermen." Turning to Mr. Stoddard, he added, "Would you and Bill mind helping me search for them?"

"Glad to," they chorused and Mr. Stoddard added, "Have you any idea where to start looking?"

Mrs. Bobbsey spoke up. "The boys were going to cruise down the shoreline to look for the bear. They promised to stay close to the beach, but perhaps they went farther than they intended. There was a stiff breeze this afternoon."

"That's it!" Mr. Bobbsey exclaimed. "The

breeze carried them down the shore, but they couldn't fight it all the way back. I'll bet they beached the raft and started home on foot. If we spread out near the shore and walk in the direction they sailed, we'll probably meet them."

"I want to hunt for my brothers too," Flossie announced.

"So do I," Nan said. "Couldn't we all go, Mother?"

Mrs. Bobbsey turned to her husband. "What do you think, Dick? It would be pretty hard for the girls and me just to wait here, and perhaps we could be of help."

"Of course you could," Mr. Bobbsey replied with a smile. "Come on, everyone!"

Nan, Flossie, and their mother carried the dishes into the tent where they quickly stacked and washed them. Then Mrs. Bobbsey caught up several warm sweaters and jackets. The search might take longer than expected and the nights became rather cool in the forest.

Soon they were on their way, walking side by side. Mr. Bobbsey walked close to the shore, with Nan about twenty feet away. Next to her were Flossie and Mrs. Bobbsey, and about twenty feet farther inland walked Bill Stoddard, with his father at the far end, about thirty feet from his son. Altogether the line of searchers stretched more than eighty feet from the shoreline into the woods. Mr. Stoddard and

Mr. Bobbsey carried flashlights, sweeping the beams in wide arcs before them.

"Keep within calling distance at all times," Mr. Bobbsey ordered. "And if you hear anything, yell!"

Twilight deepened, and soon only the lake was catching the last rays of sunlight. In the woods it had become quite dark, but the searchers walked on, calling to the lost boys every few minutes. The flashlight beams made weird patterns on trees and brush.

Suddenly Mrs. Bobbsey stopped short and cried, "Listen! I think I hear the boys calling!"

Everyone halted and strained to hear. A moment passed, then faintly from deep in the forest came weak cries:

"Help! Help, somebody!"

CHAPTER XX

TRAPPED

AN HOUR before this, Bert and Freddie had hurried along the stream that ran into the lake.

"What was that crashing noise?" Freddie asked suddenly, clutching his brother's hand. "The bear, or those mean men?"

Both boys peered to one side, trying to look through the dim forest, but they could see nothing.

"I—I think it's the bear," Freddie said fearfully, " 'cause I didn't hear two people's footsteps. What'll we do if he's not friendly?"

"I don't think it's the bear," Bert said bravely, "because he's not likely to be out at night. Anyway, a bear makes more noise than that, and I didn't hear any growls."

"No, I didn't either," Freddie said hopefully. "And bears always growl."

Suddenly they were startled by another crashing sound. The next second, a deer leaped from the near-by underbrush and in a flash vanished into the dark woods.

"Whew!" Bert exclaimed in relief. "So that's what we heard! Come on," he urged, taking longer strides. "We must hurry back to camp. I'm getting hungry."

A few minutes later, the boys discovered a path that trailed in and out among the trees and bushes close to the lake front. They hurried along this as quickly as they could.

"Don't go so fast," Freddie begged after a while. "My legs are tired."

"Oh, I forgot you don't have as long legs as I have." Bert grinned. "We'll go a bit slower. Do you want me to carry you, Freddie?"

"I can walk all right if you don't go like a leaping goat."

As they trudged along, Freddie asked, "How far do you suppose it is back to camp?"

"Oh, a mile maybe. We'll be there in twenty minutes or so."

Ten minutes later the trail led from the shore and into the woods. Here the trees concealed the fading sun.

"It's getting darker," Freddie complained.

"Oh, well, let's pretend we're cats and can see in the dark," Bert said, trying to cheer his brother.

In silence they pushed on, now and then stumbling over rocks and branches that littered the ground. Suddenly Freddie grasped Bert's hand tightly and whispered, "There's one now!"

"One what?"

"A cat—what you said we were like. I can see his eyes!"

Freddie pointed up into a tree at the right of the path. Amid the dark leaves, Bert caught sight of two glowing yellow circles. Then the yellowish lights moved and the leaves rustled.

"Maybe it's the bobcat and he's going to jump down on us!" Freddie whimpered with fear.

Bert, too, thought this might happen and quickly dragged Freddie back along the path. But all at once the stillness of the forest was broken by a loud "Hoo-hoo-too hoo!"

Freddie would have dashed away, pulling Bert after him, but the older boy stood still and chuckled.

"Aren't you scared?" Freddie demanded.

"Of course not," Bert replied. "That was only an owl and he's as frightened as we are. See! There he goes."

As Bert spoke, a shadow flitted over their heads. It was the owl flying quietly away.

A few minutes later the boys reached an open place in the woods. It was a bit lighter here, and they could see the last of the sunset, as well as the rising moon. But as they crossed the glade, something like a black dart swished close to their heads.

"There's that owl again," Freddie whispered.

"That was a bat," Bert corrected him.

"You mean like the bat that got in Flossie's room?" Freddie asked, trying to get a glimpse.

"Yes."

"Will he hurt us?"

"Not a bit," Bert said. "He's only after mosquitoes and bugs that fly after dark."

"How can he see to catch them?" Freddie wanted to know.

Bert explained that bats are equipped with a sixth sense which acts like radar.

"You mean they can always tell when something's in their way?" Freddie said, amazed.

"Always. Even in the darkest night," Bert replied.

"I wish I could do that," said Freddie. "Then we'd get home faster."

"We'll be there in a short time," Bert consoled him, but he had an uneasy feeling that they were going away from camp rather than toward it. Nevertheless, he said:

"Come on! Make believe we're soldiers, Freddie, and have to capture the enemy."

This gave Freddie a new idea to think about and he quickened his pace. In fact, he pressed on a few yards ahead of his brother.

"Don't run away from me!" Bert said, when suddenly Freddie screamed and dropped out of sight.

"Freddie! Where are you?" Bert said, groping his way forward.

There was not a sound. It seemed to him as though the younger twin had been swallowed up by the night itself. Bert dropped down on his hands and knees and felt along the ground. All at once he realized that the earth was slipping out under him. He plunged into a deep hole!

For a few moments Bert lay stunned alongside his brother. Finally catching his breath, he said, "Freddie, are you all right?"

"Y-yes," came the weak reply. "But it hurt when the ground came up and hit me!"

Bert had to chuckle in spite of their predicament.

"Freddie, we fell into a deep hole," he explained, as both boys sat up and looked above them.

The four walls of the pit were steep and at least ten feet high. They were sitting on piles of dried leaves which had been blown into the pit. Fortunately these leaves had broken the impact of their fall.

"Boy, we're going to have some time trying to climb out of here," Bert said, dropping down on the pile of leaves.

"Is this a bear's home?" Freddie asked.

"I don't think so," his brother replied. "But it might be a bear trap. Maybe the circus people dug it in order to capture Bobo."

"Let's try and climb out," Freddie suggested.

He felt around the walls for a foothold. But he succeeded only in pulling down loose dirt.

"I think we can get out if you stand on my shoulders," Bert proposed.

He lifted his brother up to a piggie-back position. Then Freddie gingerly put one foot on Bert's shoulder, then the other. He teetered for a moment, bracing himself against the dirt wall of the pit.

"Can you reach the top?" Bert called.

Freddie stretched as high as he could, but his fingertips were a foot short of the ground level.

"I can't make it," the little boy groaned.

"Stand on your tiptoes," Bert encouraged him.

When Freddie did this, he fell over backwards and landed in the leaves on the bottom of the pit.

"Oh, I bumped myself," he wailed, and started to cry.

Bert rubbed the boy's bruised legs and said, "I have an idea, Freddie. Let's dig some dirt from the bottom of the pit and pile it up against the wall. This may raise me high enough so you can reach the top."

The hope for success dried Freddie's tears. Both boys set about scooping up dirt in their hands and piling it against one of the walls of the pit.

"There," Bert said finally, "now let's try it again."

Once more he raised his brother to his shoulders, but he could feel Freddie's legs shaking from weakness. The little fellow did his best to reach the top of the pit, and once his fingers did cling to the edge. But Freddie did not have the strength to pull himself up.

"Well, I guess that's that," Bert said sadly, as his brother dropped to the ground again, and to himself, he added, "We're trapped!"

"We'll have to stay here all night," the younger lad sighed. "And nothing to eat. I wish we hadn't lost that hamper."

"I hate to have Mother and Dad worry about us all night," Bert said. "Let's call out for help now."

Freddie thought that if they cried out it might attract the suspected lumbermen. "Then they'll know where we are," he said.

"I guess we'll have to take that chance," Bert answered.

Both boys started to shout for help at the top of their lungs. The only answer was a faint echo. But a moment later the brothers realized they must have disturbed the owl, for he began to hoot. This was the only response to their cries.

"I guess nobody is near enough to hear us," Bert said finally. "Maybe you're right, Freddie. We'd better sleep here until morning."

"I'm going to shout once more," Freddie said bravely. "Help! Help, somebody!" he cried.

"Hello! Hello!" suddenly came a reply.

"What was that?" Bert asked excitedly.

"Maybe just the owl again," Freddie said.

"Owls don't say hello," Bert declared, and he called out, too.

Again the reply came. This time a woman's voice called, "Bert! Freddie! Where are you?"

"It's Mother!" the boys said happily. They set up such a din of shouting that before long they saw a light flash above them.

"We're down in a hole!" Bert shouted. "Don't fall in!"

"Thank goodness we've found you," Mrs. Bobbsey said, leaning over the opening.

Then came the sound of other voices as the Bobbsey family, along with Bill and his father, called down into the pit. Explanations were quickly given by Bert and Freddie.

"We'll have you out in a jiffy," Mr. Bobbsey said.

He yanked up a slender sapling which was growing near by and slid one end of it into the hole.

"Grab it, boys, and we'll pull you out!" he ordered.

Freddie was the first one to be hauled up, then Bert followed. What shouts of joy filled the woods as the two were hugged and kissed by their family!

"You don't seem any the worse for your adventure," Mr. Bobbsey said, throwing an arm around each of his sons. "Let's get home now. I'll bet you could stand some hot chocolate."

"More'n that," said Freddie.

"I could eat a big meal, too," Bert added, "but we have something to tell you first."

He related how he and Freddie had spied on Grimes and Lanyard around the campfire.

"If we hurry back," Bert said, "we might be able to capture them."

"Good idea. Let's go!" Mr. Stoddard said. "They dare not oppose a constable!"

Overjoyed by their release and the excitement which lay ahead, Freddie and Bert led the party back along the trail they had taken.

"We're getting close," Bert said after a while, "but the fire's out."

Talking ceased and Mr. Stoddard cautioned them to turn off their flashlights, as the searchers advanced.

"Here's the place now," Freddie whispered, as they came to a clearing.

"But nobody's around," Mr. Bobbsey said, walking over to a pile of embers that once had been the lumbermen's campfire.

"They've gone!" Freddie wailed, disappointed.

"And we wouldn't know where to trail them in the dark," Mrs. Bobbsey stated.

Her husband nodded. "Our flashlights aren't powerful enough to pick out their footprints."

"I wonder where they went," Nan said.

Her remark suddenly gave Bert an idea. He told of the canoe and of finding Mr. Bobbsey's jacket and pocketknife in it. "The canoe was named *Hide-a-way,*" the boy said.

"*Hide-a-way!*" Bill exclaimed. "Why, there's a cabin in the woods by that name."

"I'll bet a cookie the canoe belongs to the cabin!" Nan cried. "Maybe those men are hiding in it!"

"Well, it's a wonderful clue," Mr. Bobbsey said. "Do you know the way there, Bill?"

"Sure do!" Bill said.

"Then on to *Hide-a-way!*" Bert Bobbsey shouted.

CHAPTER XXI

SOLVING A RIDDLE

"HURRAY, we're going to the robbers' hideout!" Freddie cried out, at the same time rubbing his eyes with a chubby fist.

"Can you stay awake that long, little fat fireman?" his father teased.

"Sure I can, Daddy, 'specially if we're going to capture the bad men."

"I'm not sleepy, either. Honest," Flossie spoke up, as she stifled a big yawn.

"We'll piggie-back you young twins," Mr. Stoddard said, lifting Freddie to his back. Mr. Bobbsey did the same to Flossie, who flung her arms about his neck.

But before they had gone a dozen paces, Dill said, "Oh, oh, my flashlight's getting weak."

He stopped, opened the back of his torch, removed the two batteries and reversed them, in an effort to get more light. But the bulb continued to shine dimly.

"My light is going dead, too," Mr. Stoddard said ruefully.

"This means the end of our search tonight," the twins' father declared. "We can't go on without strong lights."

"Please, Dad," Bert begged. "The men may be gone by tomorrow."

"I don't think so," Mr. Stoddard put in. "It's not easy to get out of these woods after dark. Suppose we all go home and start out early tomorrow."

"Right after dawn?" Bert suggested.

"The earlier the better," Mr. Bobbsey said.

Nan and Bill were eager to join them. Mr. Bobbsey turned to put the question to the younger twins. Both were sound asleep on the backs of the two men!

"I'm sure they won't mind waiting till tomorrow," Mrs. Bobbsey smiled as she patted Flossie's curls.

Bill's flashlight now had gone out completely, so the party threaded its way back by moonlight. Arriving at the camp, Mrs. Bobbsey put Freddie and Flossie on their cots, then thanked the Stoddards for their help. As Bill and his father climbed into their farm truck, they promised to return at sunup.

"I have a feeling we'll catch those ruffians," the farmer said as he switched on his headlights and started the motor. "Good-by till morning!"

It seemed to Bert that he had no sooner put his head to the pillow when his mother was rousing him and Freddie.

"Wake up, boys," she said. "It's morning and we have to start out very soon."

As they were finishing breakfast, the Bobbseys heard the sound of the Stoddards' truck coming down the road.

"All set for the round-up?" Bill asked Bert as he opened the door and jumped to the ground.

"We're ready," Bert replied.

The twins noticed that Mr. Stoddard was wearing a constable's badge on his blue denim shirt. When he saw the others looking at it, he said:

"This shows I'm an officer of the law." Then he pulled another badge from his pocket and pinned it on Mr. Bobbsey. "I'm swearing you in as assistant constable," he added. "Now Grimes and Lanyard won't dare oppose us."

The twins felt very proud that their father was now an officer of the law, even though it would be for only a short time. What a thrilling story they would have to tell their schoolmates in Lakeport when they returned!

"Well, who's going on the search?" Mr. Stoddard asked.

"All of us," Flossie said. "Me too."

The others laughed and Mr. Stoddard said, "All right then, forward march! Bill, guide us to *Hide-a-way!*"

Bill set off on a trot, with Bert at his side. Mrs. Bobbsey followed with Freddie, Flossie, and Nan, while the two men brought up the rear.

"I know a short cut to the place," Bill told Bert, "but it's over rough territory. Do you suppose your mother and the little twins will mind?"

"Not at all," Bert replied. "They're good hikers."

Freddie and Flossie had been thoroughly refreshed by a sound night's sleep, and skipped along the way like a pair of frisky young mountain goats.

"*Hide-a-way* is in a valley on the other side of that hill," Bill said, pointing to a steep wooded slope ahead of them. This word was passed along the line, and everyone quickened his pace.

The hill was so steep that the hikers had to grasp bushes and saplings to help make their way to the top. Reaching the summit, they stopped to catch their breath.

Below them lay a valley carpeted with deep green foliage. Near the middle of it the Bobbseys could see a small clearing through which ran a good-sized stream. And on the banks of the stream was a low, sprawling cabin.

"That's it!" Bill said excitedly.

"Look!" Freddie exclaimed. "Smoke is coming out of the chimney. The bad men are home!"

"We'll surround the cabin and capture

them!" Freddie declared, throwing out his chest.

"Everybody must be very quiet," Mr. Bobbsey warned as they set off, this time with the men in the lead, Mrs. Bobbsey and the girls in the rear. "No talking when we reach *Hide-a-way*. The men might run off if they hear us."

Traveling downhill Indian file, he cautioned the children not to step on brittle branches nor make any other kind of noise.

Ahead of them the cabin now was visible among the trees. Mr. Bobbsey beckoned everybody to stop.

"From here in we'll advance from tree to tree," he whispered, "so they won't see us. I want Bill and Bert to station themselves at the back of the cabin in case anyone tries to escape that way. Mr. Stoddard and I will approach the front door and arrest them."

"What can the rest of us do?" Nan asked.

"You shout as loudly as you can if the men try to escape."

"Why, Daddy?" Flossie asked.

"They'll think a whole posse's after them and might give up right away," he explained.

Bert and Bill dodged from tree to tree until they were behind a fallen trunk at the rear of the cabin.

"Look, there's a back door," Bert whispered to his friend.

At the front, meanwhile, Mr. Bobbsey and

Mr. Stoddard had stepped into the clearing and strode to the main door of *Hide-a-way*.

Mr. Bobbsey rapped loudly but nobody answered. "Grimes and Lanyard, if you are inside, come out!" he shouted.

"You're under arrest!" Mr. Stoddard added. "You can't get away because we have you surrounded!"

Still nobody came to the door. But the two men suddenly heard muffled shouts from back of the cabin.

"Stay here and guard this door, Stoddard!" Mr. Bobbsey said, and raced around the side of the building.

He arrived at the rear of it just in time to see two men dash toward the woods. The wanted lumbermen! But as they passed the fallen log, Bert and Bill sprang out and tackled them. The two fellows fell to the ground with jolting thuds.

"Stoddard! Here they are!" Mr. Bobbsey cried. The farmer came running, and together he and Mr. Bobbsey helped collar the fugitives.

Grimes and Lanyard stood up, scowling. "What do you want?" Grimes growled.

"You're bad men," accused Freddie, who had run up, " 'cause you stole things from our blown-down bungalow."

"We can explain everything," Lanyard said.

"Let's hear your story," Mr. Bobbsey prodded.

The story that unfolded was indeed a strange
one. The prisoners said that after talking to
Mr. Bobbsey, they had gone again to Mr.
Wadell for their wages. He had insisted that
Mr. Bobbsey would pay them.

"But Mr. Wadell was to pay you himself!"
Mr. Bobbsey explained. "If you're telling the
truth, it seems to me that Wadell is trying to
pull a fast trick."

The two men then went on to explain that
they had gone to call on Mr. Bobbsey a few
hours after the storm had blown down their
cottage.

"We were angry not to find you there so we
could get our pay," Grimes said. "We thought
you had left the cottage for good. That's why
we took the things."

"We're not thieves," Lanyard put in. "We'll
give back everything we took. It's all in the
shack, except the jacket we lost in the canoe
and a cap that disappeared."

He then told Mr. Bobbsey that he had laid
the jacket in the canoe, but had not tied the
craft securely enough.

"It got away from us," he said ruefully.

"And we found it," Freddie said proudly.

"The name *Hide-a-way* was what led us to
your cabin," Bert added.

Mr. Bobbsey in turn said that he was sorry
for the mix-up about payment for the lumbering job. "I'll have a talk with Wadell and see

that he pays you as soon as possible," he said.

Mr. Stoddard nodded. "Then I guess it won't be necessary to arrest anybody today," the constable said.

"It sure has been a queer day for us," Lanyard said with a wry grin. "Just before you came, a bear nearly scared the daylights out of us."

"A bear?" the children chorused.

"Yes," Grimes said, rubbing his wrists. "The big fellow lumbered into our cabin and took a bundle of clothes right off my bunk."

"Did he hurt you?" Flossie asked.

"No, he didn't," the man answered. "But he did something awful peculiar."

"What was that?" Bert queried.

"You won't believe it," Lanyard said with an embarrassed grin, "but this bear wrapped the clothes around himself and started to dance!"

"It was Bobo!" Flossie shouted.

"Friend of yours?" Lanyard asked in surprise.

The twins then told the story of the lost trick bear that belonged to a circus.

"Where did he go?" Bert asked excitedly.

"He dashed out of the cabin and went into the woods right about here," Grimes said, pointing.

Suddenly Nan shouted, "I see the bear's tracks! Let's find Bobo!"

CHAPTER XXII

AN AMUSING FAREWELL

NAN'S CRY that she had found the bear tracks brought her family and the Stoddards on the run. Together they examined the prints, then Bert said:

"Please, Dad, may we follow them? I'm sure Bobo hasn't gone far since he raided this cabin, and we'll never have a better chance to capture him. Please!"

With a twinkle in her eyes, Nan held up the repaired collar and chain from the Empire Circus.

"Where did you get that?" Mr. Bobbsey asked, chuckling.

"I brought it along when we started for the cabin," Nan replied. "I thought we might run into Bobo, so just in case—"

Mrs. Bobbsey laughed. "What determined children!" she exclaimed. "Poor Bobo is as good as captured already!"

"As long as we've come this far," Mr. Bobbsey said, "we may as well finish the job and round up the bear, too."

"I don't think Freddie and Flossie had bet- ter go," Mrs. Bobbsey said. "Suppose I stay with them, Dick, while you and Nan and Bert go bear hunting."

Mr. Stoddard offered to stay also. Secretly he wanted to keep track of Grimes and Lanyard. But Bill was eager to join the search.

"All right," Mr. Bobbsey said. "Come along."

The group started off, following the distinct imprints in the sand along the stream. Bert took the lead, carrying the collar and chain.

They had walked in silence for perhaps a quarter of a mile, when Bert stopped short and gasped, "The prints stop here! No sign of them anywhere ahead."

"But Bobo couldn't evaporate," Nan declared.

She had hardly said this when suddenly two sparkling brown eyes peeped around a tree at Bert's side. Before anyone could cry out, a big black paw whipped out and snatched the collar and chain.

Then out stepped Bobo, swinging the collar around his head and tossing it up in the air. The chain spun crazily, then *smack!* The trick bear caught the collar smartly in both paws.

He turned it around slowly, his bright eyes seeming to study the collar carefully. For a second Bobo seemed puzzled, then with a snort he put it on his head and pushed down hard.

Out stepped Bobo, swinging the collar around his head

Everyone roared with laughter and clapped. Instantly Bobo bowed to his audience, doffing the collar like a hat.

At that moment, Nan signaled Bert and the two cautiously approached the bear. Bobo *whoofed* when Nan touched the collar, but remained quiet as she unfastened the catch and slipped the leather around his neck. Once it was on and securely fastened, Bert pulled lightly on the chain. Without protest, the bear followed him.

"Well, that was certainly easy!" Mr. Bobbsey exclaimed, quietly drawing a deep breath in relief. "Bobo seems almost glad to be with people again. And say, here's my hunting cap!"

The children's father picked up the bright red cap from the sand. But just as he started to put it on his head, Bobo snatched it away, hugging the cap against his big chest.

"I guess it's Bobo's cap now," Nan said, smiling, and the bear promptly clapped it on his head. Mr. Bobbsey shrugged good-naturedly, and the little troupe set off.

Upon reaching the cabin, they found that Grimes and Lanyard had all the clothes and food ready to cart back to the Bobbsey tent.

When Flossie saw the bear, she squealed with delight and ran to him. "I'm sorry I screamed that time and scared you, Bobo," she said.

"Careful, Flossie!" Mr. Bobbsey cried, but he was too late.

*The little girl had already been caught up
in Bobo's big paws!*

Up, up, she went until she was high above
the bear's head. White-faced, her family
watched, afraid to speak. A warning cry now
might startle Bobo, then anything might happen!

But, gently, the bear lowered Flossie and set
her safely on the ground. The little girl hugged
him around the knees. "I think you're just awful nice!" she said.

"The feeling seems to be mutual," Mr. Bobbsey said with a relieved chuckle. "Well, I guess
we're ready to start back now."

Mr. Stoddard and Bill left for their own
home. The Bobbseys and Bobo started back to
their tent with Grimes and Lanyard. Bert, Nan,
and Freddie took turns leading Bobo by his
chain, but Flossie skipped along beside her
new friend.

When they reached the tent, Nan and Mrs.
Bobbsey prepared a quick but hearty lunch
for the family and Grimes and Lanyard. Mr.
Bobbsey said he was going to town, and promised the twins that he would call the manager
of the Empire Circus immediately to tell him
of Bobo's capture.

"I'll ask him to meet us in town tomorrow,"
he said.

Following lunch, Mr. Bobbsey left with the
lumbermen to see Mr. Wadell in the distant

city and straighten out the mix-up over the
men's pay. The twins helped their mother with
the work about the camp, then everyone, even
Bobo, went for a swim.

After splashing about happily with the children, the bear wandered a little way down the
shore and waded into the water until it was
about waist deep. He stood perfectly still, staring under the ripples. Then, with a lightning-
quick movement, his paw scooped deep into
the water and came up clutching a fish.

"Oh, isn't he wonderful?" Flossie said
proudly, and everyone agreed.

"I wish I could catch a trout that way," Bert
laughed.

About four o'clock he suggested that he and
Nan take Bobo for a walk. They might visit
the Stoddards and perhaps ask Bill to drive
them to town the next day in the farm truck.
If the circus manager agreed to meet them,
they would need some transportation other
than the family car. Bobo just would not fit
into the back seat—at least not with the twins
occupying it, too!

When Nan and Bert reached the Stoddard
farm, thick gray clouds were forming on the
horizon. The air was muggy and stifling, and
the twins were very hot. Mrs. Stoddard invited
the twins into her kitchen for some lemonade,
although she seemed rather uneasy about having a large bear on her back porch!

Bill came in from the barn a few moments later and Bert told him of the plan to deliver Bobo the next day. He asked if Bill would drive them to town in his truck.

"Why, sure," the good-natured youth replied. "Wouldn't miss it for the world." He grinned. "The kids in town will talk about it for months!"

After Bobo had been given a pan of cool water, the twins thanked Mrs. Stoddard and started back to the camp.

"It's getting sort of dark," Bert remarked, as he and Nan entered the woods with Bobo. "It's sure going to storm."

By the time the twins reached the tent, the sky was completely overcast and whitecaps frosted the lead-colored lake.

"Hi!" Nan called, as her mother came out of the tent to greet them. "Is Dad back yet? We want to tell him about the truck."

"Not yet," Mrs. Bobbsey replied, "but I'm sure he will be soon. I hope he gets here before the rain starts. Why don't you and Bert give Bobo some supper and then put him in the car shed for the night? He'll be dry in there and it won't hurt our car to stand out."

Flossie and Freddie wanted to help, so the four children fixed nuts, cereal, and raspberry jam for the bear's meal. Then they led him inside the shed.

Flossie wagged her finger at him. "Now don't

you be scared, Bobo," she said reassuringly. "The rain can't get you here."

Bobo *whoofed* in reply and began to play with a red ball Freddie had given him.

As the children were returning to the tent, Mr. Bobbsey drove up the trail. Grimes and Lanyard were not with him.

The twins ran to greet their father and explain why the car would have to remain outside all night. Just then the rain started.

"Hey!" Mr. Bobbsey exclaimed. "Let's get under cover."

Bert and Freddie helped him roll up the car windows, then they all dashed to the tent. Mrs. Bobbsey held open the front flap and they scurried inside. How cozy it seemed with the rain pelting on the taut canvas top!

"Did Mr. Wadell pay the lumbermen?" Bert asked presently, and Nan cried, "Will the circus manager meet us tomorrow?"

Mr. Bobbsey laughed. "One at a time! First, Wadell paid the men immediately when I told him who I was and what had happened. He said he was not making much on the deal. He had hoped to get off without paying the men by telling them I owed them their wages.

"Knowing that my mill was some distance away, he figured I would pay the men to avoid trouble and to get the lumber."

"I'm glad everything is straightened out," Mrs. Bobbsey said.

"And what about the circus manager and Bobo?" Flossie persisted excitedly.

"It's all arranged," her father replied. "Mr. Hoffman—that's the manager's name—was delighted that you had found Bobo. He'll meet us in town tomorrow at eleven and is making arrangements to send Bobo on to the circus by train. But the question is, how are we to get Bobo into town?"

Bert and Nan grinned as they told of the arrangements they had made with Bill Stoddard.

The conversation was interrupted by a shout of, "Hey, Mr. Bobbsey!" from outside the tent. It was Sam Todd, dressed in a slicker and rain cap. "Everything is all set, Mr. Bobbsey," he said. "We plan to tie the rafts together tomorrow at dawn and start the trip to your mill. That is," he added, "if the rain lets up."

"Fine!" Mr. Bobbsey exclaimed. "I'm sure the weather will clear. And in fact, I guess all our business here will be finished by that time." Turning to his family, he said, "Shall we plan to pack up and go home tomorrow?"

The children were reluctant to leave their lovely camping spot. But they agreed that there were many things to do at home before school started. So after Mr. Todd left, the family packed most of their belongings, leaving out only the clothes and food they would need for the following morning.

Next day the Bobbseys awoke to beautiful

sunny skies. The woods looked scrubbed and shining after the rain, and the lake was the bluest they had ever seen it. How hard it was to leave such a spot!

The lumbermen on their string of huge rafts were already far from shore. After waving good-by to them, the children had a hearty breakfast, then scurried about helping with the final packing and cleaning. Mr. Bobbsey had arranged for men from town to dismantle the tent and ship it back to the rental agency after his family had gone.

About nine o'clock Bill drove up in the farm truck. He had put the slatted sides on to keep Bobo from leaping out. The bear was led up a plank onto the back of the truck. He hunched down and peered mischievously at the children through the slats.

Laughing, the twins clambered onto the truck with their captive and Bill took the wheel. After stowing the remaining supplies in the car, Mr. and Mrs. Bobbsey started off, following the farm truck.

What a gay time the children had all the way to town! Bobo entertained them with tricks and danced with each of the children. As they drove down the main street of town, people on the sidewalk exclaimed in surprise at the sight.

In the center of the town, Mr. Hoffman, the circus manager, awaited them. When the truck stopped, Bobo swung Flossie up and around and made a sweeping bow to the crowd of people who were watching.

Mr. Hoffman thanked the children profusely, and told them that each of the twins and also Bill Stoddard could always see the Empire Circus without having to buy tickets.

"We'll be coming to Lakeport next summer," the manager said to the twins. "You'll be our guests of honor! In fact, we'd like you to be part of Bobo's act while the circus is in your town. What do you say?"

"Do—do you think he'll remember us by then?" Flossie asked wistfully. It was evident that she hated to part with their new animal friend.

"I'm sure he will," Mr. Hoffman assured her kindly. "He'll be waiting all year to dance with you children again."

"So will we!" the Bobbseys chorused.

Flossie gave Bobo a last hug, then Mr. Hoffman led him to the railroad station. But the bear, still wearing the red hunting cap, kept looking back at the children as if he, too, were sad to say good-by.

The Bobbseys waved. Then each of them shook hands with Bill. He begged them to visit the lake next summer.

"And maybe Mr. Hoffman will let us borrow Bobo for a few days," Nan said, chuckling.

"Oh, yes!" exclaimed Freddie. "He could help me catch some fish!"

Everyone laughed and the children joined their parents in the car.

As they drove away, Bert said, "That was the greatest vacation ever!"

"And just think!" Flossie exclaimed. "Daddy's cap has joined the circus!"